"We should all be proud of what it means to be an auk—simple in our ways and self-reliant, born with an innate sense of justice and a love of community. Never take your blessings, most of all your independence, for granted."

WALDEN P
AN IMPRINT OF HAR

Pre

Never

A Puf

By BARRY W

With drawings by SA

OND PRESS
RCOLLINS*PUBLISHERS*

nts

sink

n Saga

OLVERTON

M NIELSON

Walden Pond Press is an imprint of HarperCollins Publishers.
Walden Pond Press and the skipping stone logo are trademarks
and registered trademarks of Walden Media, LLC.

Library of Congress Cataloging-in-Publication Data
Wolverton, Barry.
Neversink / by Barry Wolverton ; with drawings by Sam Nielson. — 1st ed.
p. cm.
Summary: When owls threaten the puffins' way of life on the small island of Neversink along the Arctic Circle, Lockley J. Puffin, helped by a hummingbird and a walrus, sets out to save it.
ISBN 978-0-06-202793-1
[1. Puffins—Fiction. 2. Owls—Fiction. 3. Islands—Fiction. 4. War—Fiction. 5. Animals—Fiction. 6. Arctic regions—Fiction.]
I. Nielson, Sam, ill. II. Title.
PZ7.W8375Ne 2012 2011016550
[Fic]—dc23

Typography by Amy Ryan
13 14 15 16 17 OPM 10 9 8 7 6 5 4 3 2 1
❖
First paperback edition, 2013

For my mother.

Neversink, indeed.

CONTENTS

Part Two: *Over Sea, Under Ground*

Part Three: *Ocean's End*

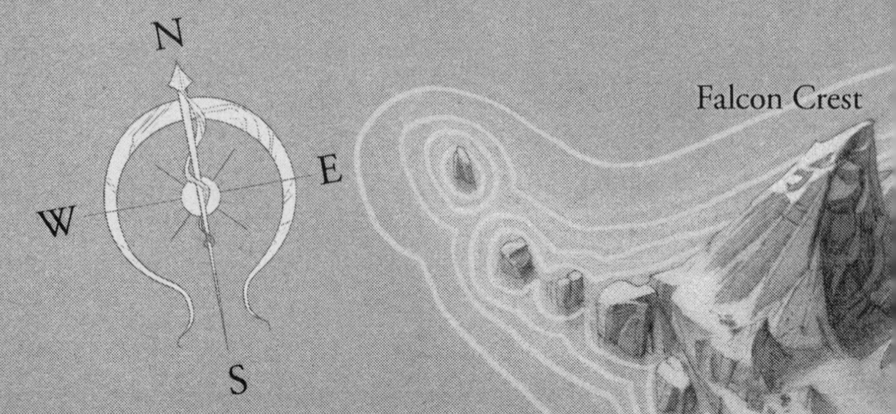
GREAT
NORTHERN
SEA
Mouth of Fire
The
Thermals
The Beach
NEVERSINK
Auk's Landing
Great Auk's Nest
Falcon Crest
N
E
W
S

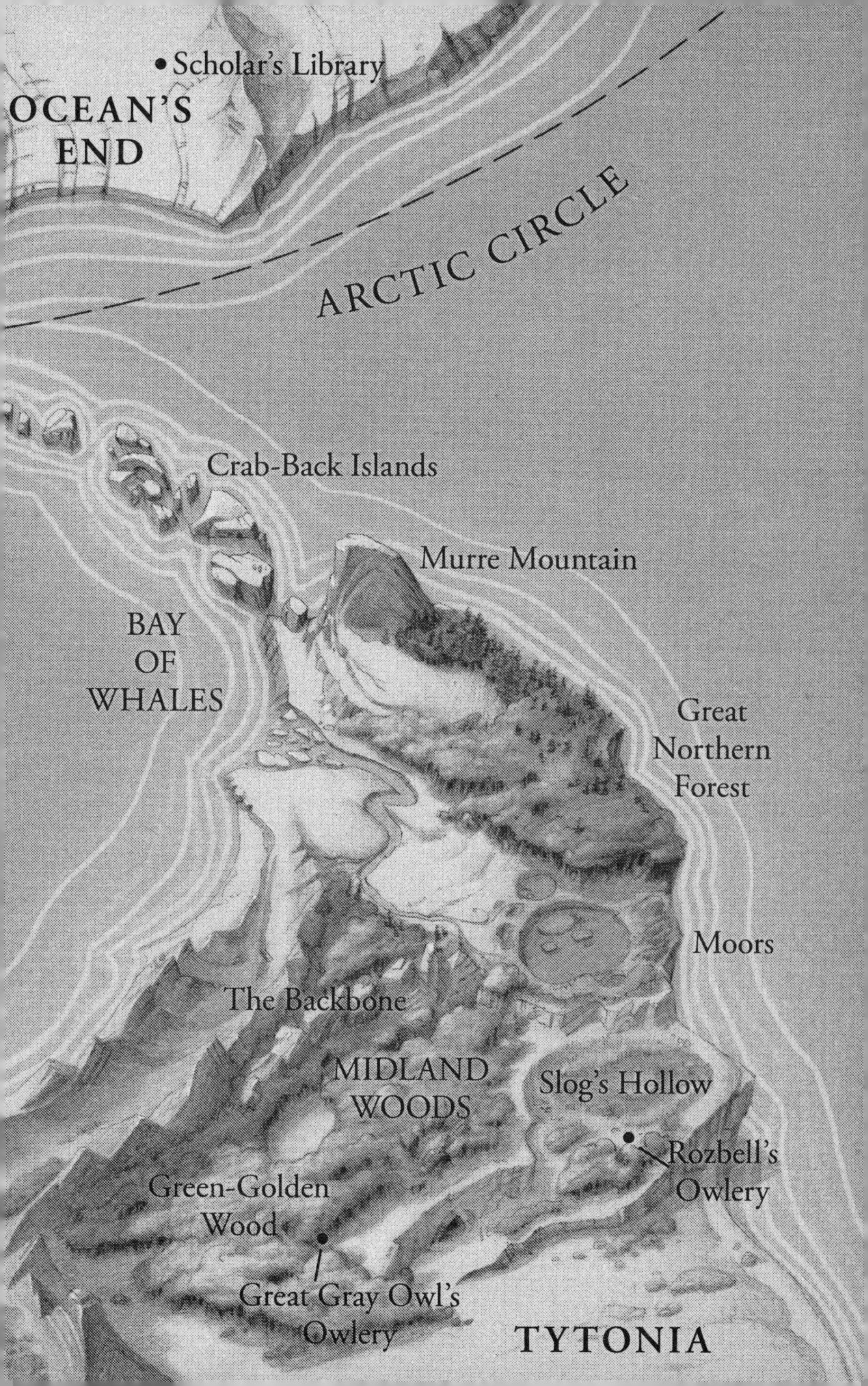

Scholar's Library

OCEAN'S END

ARCTIC CIRCLE

Crab-Back Islands

Murre Mountain

BAY OF WHALES

Great Northern Forest

Moors

The Backbone

MIDLAND WOODS

Slog's Hollow

Rozbell's Owlery

Green-Golden Wood

Great Gray Owl's Owlery

TYTONIA

Birds of the Northerly World

Excerpted from THE WALRUS GUIDE TO LESSER CREATURES, *Sixteenth Edition*

AUKS

Plump, duck-like seafarers with rapid, buzzing flight. Nest in dense, noisy, often malodorous colonies; "fly" underwater and prefer tea with their fish.

Puffin: Smallish, squidgy, improbable looking. Relatively quiet and well-mannered, except when provoked. Not to be confused with a penguin, or a parrot, or a cross between a penguin and a parrot.

Razorbill: Largest of the Neversink auks. Only one sensibly named, after its distinctive wedge-shaped bill. Creaking "*urrr*" or harsh "*arrr*" call. Renowned for skill in carving wood and ivory.

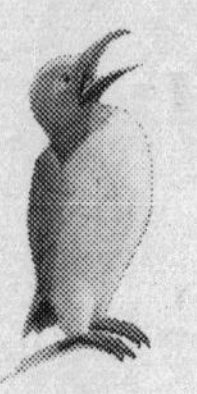

Murre: Largish, with a long narrow bill. Purrs, croaks, and growls, depending on mood; can dive more than 300 feet; nests high on cliffs, presumably out of snootiness.

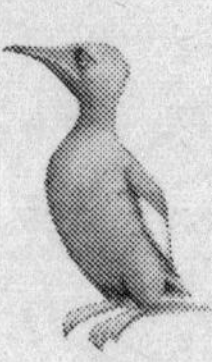

Guillemot: Medium-sized. Unnecessarily florid name. Noisy, disagreeable, with bright orange-red tongue often displayed impolitely. Grating, high-pitched "*peeee*" call.

OWLS

Mostly nocturnal birds of prey, distinguished by forward-facing eyes and legendary wisdom. May or may not have visible ear tufts, called horns. May or may not wear hats.

Snowy owl: Day-hunting white owl preferring open hunting grounds. Large, heavily feathered feet to protect from cold; yellow eyes. Cold habitat reputedly matched by cool disposition.

Pygmy owl: Smallest but most ill-tempered of Tytonian owls. Ambush hunter with undulating flight like the woodpecker's. Prone to violent outbursts, physical and verbal tics, and delusions of grandeur.

Scops owl: Tall, slender horned owl of phlegmatic humor. Resembles an overgrown moth. No idea what "scops" means.

Great gray owl: Large, dark barred owl with relatively small yellow eyes. Known for driving off predators as large as black bears when defending nest. Like many large owls, often overly self-satisfied.

Unsnack your snood, madanna, for the stars
Are shining on all brows of Neversink.

Already the green bird of summer has flown
Away.

—Wallace Stevens,
"Late Hymn From the Myrrh-Mountain"

PROLOGUE

A Most Forbidding Place (Unless You're an Auk)

If you were to follow the imaginary line known as the Arctic Circle all the way around the world, you would eventually land on a small island called Neversink, whose shores are lapped by the icy waters of the Great Northern Sea.

Not that you'd want to. Rugged and wintry, Neversink was forged by fire from an undersea volcano. The ground is like teeth and the wind lashes like a whip. The interior is a bleak landscape of glacial ice caps, ancient black basalt, and frozen soil called tundra. Wild grasslands and soggy bogs cover the warmer southern regions, but there are few trees because of the lack of rain. In summer the sun scarcely sets; in winter it scarcely rises. And volcanoes disguised as snow-capped mountains erupt without warning, carving the scarred surface anew with flowing lava.

But the jagged southern coastline, where sheer cliffs and moss-covered rocks rise above the bays and fjords, was once the perfect home for a group of seabirds known as auks. Short, stubby, black-and-white birds, all with funny-sounding names to match their funny-looking appearance: Razorbill. Murre. Guillemot. Puffin. Neversink was home to the largest population of these strange birds in that part of the world—the colony of Auk's Landing.

These are birds who happily spend much of their time at sea, eat fish, fly underwater, and are *not* to be confused with penguins. On Neversink auks could nest safely in the nooks and crannies of the island's ice-gouged rocks, far away from the perching birds of nearby Tytonia, protected from predators by a girdle of ocean, safe from most threats other than old age and an unpredictable sea goddess named Sedna.

So had it been since the Age of Settlement. And so would it have remained, many believe, if Rozbell had never tasted Lucy Puffin's fish smidgens.

But we're getting ahead of ourselves. For now, you should know that the world of this story is one that existed long ago and is no more. The continents had formed and separated but were covered with forests. The dinosaurs were long gone. Humans did not yet roam the earth, much less rule it. In short, it was a bird's paradise.

And as you may have guessed from the cover of the book, one bird in particular, once upon a time, behaved heroically enough (or foolishly enough, depending on who you ask) for someone to write about him.

Of course, you might not be reading this story at all if walruses couldn't talk. I know what you're thinking. *All* animals can talk. Some can even sing, dance, and play golf. But it was walruses, after all, who came up with the notion of converting *talking* into *writing*, so that future generations of animals could enjoy all the many wonderful things walruses have to say.

One walrus in particular was, I believe, the author of *A Short History of Neversink,* which is the source of the story I am about to tell you. How can I be so sure? I think once you read on, you will understand completely. Or not. By the end you may not remember you read this.

And why not just read *A Short History of Neversink*? Let me assure the reader that, while walruses are great scholars of the first order, they operate on a scale alien to mere humans. To a walrus, for example, to weigh less than four thousand pounds makes you "slim." And a meal of fewer than three thousand clams is a "light snack."

Along those lines, there is nothing short about *A Short History of Neversink.* (*A Short History of Neversink* is actually a multivolume set that is part of the multi-multivolume set *A Long History of the Whole World*, which would take the average human more than one hundred fifty years to read.) Despite the important research and fantastic stories contained within, the author, like all walrus authors, is given to numerous and lengthy digressions about whatever may tickle his whiskers—chiefly, the importance of food, the acquisition of food, the preparation of food, and the eating of food. There are also many passages devoted to the excellence of the walrus mind and the importance of the walrus opinion. Trust me when I tell you that most of this is of little interest to the nonwalrus.

So, consider the story in your hand a translation of sorts. I have even changed the names of some things and places to their contemporary names to help you, dear reader, better understand this strange world.

PART ONE
A Smidgen of Fish

PERCHANCE TO SOAR

At the outer reaches of Auk's Landing, there was a high, narrow ledge that jutted out over the sea and curved to a point like a sharp bill. Over the years, this isolated spot had become a kind of sanctuary for Lockley Puffin, to escape the chaos and clamor of his fellow auks.

If you know anything about puffins, you know they don't quite fit in with their seafaring kin. You see, auks as a group look very much alike, with their black-and-white plumage and webbed feet. The puffins' large, colorful bills and bright orange legs made them objects of suspicion in a colony where Blend In and Don't Make Waves were the guiding principles of life.

And even for a puffin, Lockley had a habit of sticking

out in all the wrong ways. In fact, Lockley had earned a reputation as a bit of a troublemaker.

He didn't mean to be (a troublemaker, that is). But puffins are known for being relatively quiet among the auk families—their appearance is loud enough—and so it was very noticeable when one wasn't (quiet, I mean).

Like the time the Parliament of Owls decided Neversink could no longer import cranberries from Tytonia without paying a hefty "transportation fee." Parliament, the lawmaking body of owls that governed the kingdom of Tytonia, knew how much the auks enjoyed making cranberry scones. Everyone agreed it was a brazen attempt to punish Neversink. (And for no good reason, at that.)

But only Lockley wanted to raise the issue with the Great Auk, the colony's law-speaker. Surely Parliament's actions violated the Peace of Yore—the treaty that had made Neversink an *independent* colony of Tytonia. What did it mean to be independent if, at the end of the day, you were still controlled by owls?

To the colony's dismay, the Great Auk agreed it was worthy of a vote to decide whether to protest the decree. The colony voted almost unanimously to do without cranberries. Don't Make Waves.

It was exactly this sort of unpleasantness that caused Lockley to retreat to his private place. He stood there now, looking toward the horizon. It was that time of day on

Neversink when sunrise mirrored sunset. The sun was just above the water, bruising the sky. The water was a deep, dark, humpback gray, except for a strip of light cutting a path from sun to shore, inviting Lockley to walk across it. Lockley liked to imagine that such a celestial path guided his ancestors to Neversink when they were forced to leave Tytonia.

Lockley gathered up the fish he'd caught that morning and clasped them in his bill. His wife, Lucy, would be expecting him back by now. But he had something else to attend to first. Something not even Lucy knew about. He stepped to the very edge of the precipice and shook out his wings. His breath came quickly, but it was neither owls nor auks that were agitating him. He was trying to learn how to *soar*. He was embarrassed by the buzzy, frantic flight of puffins and other auks, who had to beat their wings rapidly to keep their squash-shaped bodies above the water. Even then, they often veered wildly, tossed by the Northern Sea's wind gusts. He didn't think it was very bird-like.

It was bad enough to be awkward on land. Lots of seabirds were. But the albatross, the petrel, and the sea eagle, once airborne, all circled high toward the sun, coasting on thermal updrafts, gliding on the wing. How wonderful it would be to float above the sea and enjoy the solitude of the heavens. Lockley wanted to be like them, a sky roamer.

And so, his heart beating even more fiercely than his wings, Lockley put his feet together and launched himself from the cliff, toward the sky. Up and up he went, until he felt the thermals beneath him . . . lifting him . . . carrying him. He stopped flapping, spread his wings wide, and began to coast with effortless power. It was a thrilling sensation. Until, as always, doubt weighed him down. Doubt that said, *Puffins aren't meant to soar.*

And slowly, slowly, he began to fall.

North of Auk's Landing, Neversink's towering sea cliffs gave way to sloping lava fields, tide pools surrounded by tiny islands of black rock, and flat stretches of sand that the seals and seabirds called the beach.

Now, if the word *beach* brings to mind tropical postcards or warm summer vacations, think again. Picture instead a shoreline that looks like the colossal warty foot of a giant dipping his toes in the ocean. And standing on this scarred and rocky ground was an especially large walrus, looking with some concern at an object in the sky while a frenetic hummingbird darted back and forth from one side of his head to the other.

"What do you think it is, Egbert?" (into his left ear). "A comet?" (into his right ear). "An asteroid?"

"Hardly."

The flying object came nearer . . . a dark projectile,

tumbling, wobbling, hurtling recklessly through the air.

"Is it a bird, Egbert?" asked the hummingbird.

"Doesn't look like any bird I've seen," the walrus patiently replied.

"Is it a plane?"

"There's no such thing as a plane!"

"Is it a flying sack of onions?"

"Ruby, there is *no such thing* as a flying sack of—"

And in that moment of distraction, it crashed. Right into Egbert, to be precise. There was a sound like a cannonball hitting mashed potatoes as the flying object collided with a mound of walrus flesh, bounced to the ground, and rolled to a lumpy stop.

"Lockley! Good heavens!" said Egbert. "Are you okay?"

Lockley sat up, dazed. He shook his head from side to side until the giant walrus and the tiny hummingbird came into focus.

"I think you bruised one of my ribs!" said Egbert, rubbing his side.

"There are bones under there?" said Ruby.

Lockley wobbled to his feet. "Terribly sorry, Egbert. I didn't see you there."

"You're kidding, right?" said Ruby. But Lockley ignored her as he cleaned up his mess. The fish he'd been carrying had scattered all over the rocks, and as he gathered them up, he plopped them into an enclosed tide pool, where there was already a school of small, silvery fish known as sand eels—a favorite of puffins.

Egbert peered into the pool. "Lockley, are you eating fish or collecting them?"

"Both!" said Lockley. "What I mean is, they're not just for Lucy and me."

"Are they for me?" said Egbert, his whiskers twitching with excitement.

"Are they for me?" said Ruby.

"Hummingbirds don't eat fish," Egbert shot back.

"Oh, yeah."

"They don't customarily live near Ocean's End, either," Egbert reminded her.

"They aren't for either of you," said Lockley. Egbert shrank with disappointment, before Lockley added, "Not directly, anyway. Egbert—Lucy has agreed to make her world-famous fish smidgens for your surprise birthday party!"

"Really?" said Egbert.

"Surprise!"

"What's so surprising?" Ruby asked. "Egbert planned the whole thing himself!"

Egbert struggled to maintain his composure. "Dear, dear Lockley. You and Lucy are such dear, dear friends."

"Come to think of it," said Ruby, "how did you get the whole colony to agree to come to your party?"

Egbert righted himself and said, "I simply explained to them that I planned to reveal something that will dramatically change all their lives for the better."

"Oh, right," said Ruby. "You lied to them."

"I did not lie to them!" said Egbert, and he was prepared to defend himself with great gusto, when suddenly he turned to Lockley and gave him a critical look—the kind of look that usually preceded one of his lectures. "Lockley, why were you flying like that?"

"Like what?" said Lockley, fidgeting.

"Like you were launched out of a catapult," said Ruby.

"There's no such thing as a catapult," said Lockley.

"Lockley . . . you were trying to *soar* again," said Egbert, pointing an accusing fin at him.

"I don't know what you're talking about."

"You could have broken your neck hitting these rocks from that high up!" Egbert scolded.

"Good thing there was a million pounds of blubber here to break your fall," said Ruby.

"I am quite normal-sized for a walrus!" Egbert bellowed.

Lockley sighed as his friends fell to bickering again. Unlike puffins, Egbert and Ruby seemed to enjoy sticking out, and one was never happy if the other was commanding too much attention. Egbert, after all, was the only walrus on Neversink. Most of his kin lived in large clans near the North Pole. He claimed to be on a mission to spread the walrus gifts of learning to the rest of the world, Neversink being his first stop. The auks had long ago given up hope that he would ever leave.

Ruby was even more of a stranger. Her family was from what humans would call the New World (it was new to them, anyway). South America, to be exact. While migrating north one summer, she was blown off course and forced to make a rest stop on Neversink. Lockley and Egbert had never seen such a curious thing, and their attention was like sugar water to the proud little hummingbird. Now Ruby summered there every year, sustained by the wildflowers that grew on the grasslands during this milder season.

In a colony where Blend In was an unwritten rule (well, all rules were unwritten before the Age of Writing), you can imagine what most auks thought of Egbert and Ruby. Naturally, Lockley was an exception. He and Lucy thought it made life a little more interesting to have these fellow misfits around. A coastline full of black-and-white seabirds could get a bit monotonous.

And even though Lockley had never taken to this idea of reading and writing, he had become quite fond of Egbert over the years, and Ruby too. If he occasionally grew short with their bickering, it was only because he felt protective of them, and wanted to keep them from irritating the other auks so much.

"Don't start, you two," he said. "You don't want me to lose my temper!"

Egbert and Ruby stopped arguing, each drawing a mental picture of an angry puffin. They both burst out laughing.

"Stop that," said Lockley, as the laughter continued. "Stop laughing this instant if you want smidgens at your party." Egbert abruptly fell silent. "Good, now if you'll help me gather these fish up, I'll put them all in a seaweed net and take them to Lucy."

Egbert helped Lockley bundle up the fish while Ruby supervised. "Lockley?" she said. "Are you sure Lucy can even cook all those smidgens? Especially if she has to make enough for the mainlanders?"

Lockley got that feeling in his throat like when he accidentally inhaled an oyster. Summer was breeding season on Auk's Landing, and he and Lucy were expecting their first piffling (the puffin word for *child*). Two summers ago, she had fallen ill and lost her egg. Then last year, the volcano the birds called the Mouth of Fire rumbled and collapsed their burrow. It was their habit to dig burrows into the ground rather than live higher up on the cliffs like other auks. They were less exposed to egg-snatching seabirds this way—but it left them exposed to other dangers. Many puffins lost their eggs the day the earth shook.

That said, Lockley had begun to take their bad luck

personally. He was determined not to let *anything* happen to either Lucy or their egg this time. Even if it meant plugging the Mouth of Fire (*perhaps with Egbert,* he thought, watching his enormous friend sweep fish into the net with his forefins). After making such a promise to himself, was it possible he was already failing Lucy?

Then, something else Ruby had said jarred him. "You invited the mainlanders?" Lockley asked Egbert. That was what the birds of Neversink called the creatures of Tytonia.

"How can such a small bird have such a big mouth?" Egbert wondered aloud.

"I suppose as long as you didn't invite the owls," said Lockley.

Ruby was on the verge of blurting something out when Egbert swatted her away.

"Egbert, in the name of Sedna, you didn't! You know how things are between auks and owls!" That was Egbert's problem. He always meant well, but he didn't always consider the consequences of his actions. It was just the sort of thing that kept him on the bad side of most of the auks.

Lost in thought, Lockley wandered to the shoreline and stared across the sea in the direction of Tytonia, domain of the owls. On either end of thick forests rose two peaks—to the south was Falcon Crest; to the north, Murre Mountain, former home of the auks, until the Cod Wars had led to their exile from Tytonia and relocation to Neversink.

This had all happened long before Lockley's time. But he often wondered what it would be like to live on Tytonia. It was also an island, but much larger. It was sunnier and warmer, too, a half-day's flight southeast of Neversink. Trees, grasses, and flowers of great variety flourished there, so that beasts and birds of all kinds could find their habitat. Under the current political arrangement, owls could not even visit Neversink without a direct invitation from a member of the colony. Needless to say, those weren't often handed out. But if Egbert had invited them . . . well, he just might have opened a can of worms (which for birds is normally a good thing, but not in this case).

"Yoo-hoo! Zombie puffin!" It was Ruby, hovering right in front of his face. "If Lucy's gonna get cookin', we better get crackin'!"

"Yes, right," Lockley agreed. He threw the net of fish over his shoulder, the extra burden threatening to topple him right over, until the great weight was lifted off him. It was Egbert, grabbing the net and carrying it himself.

"Thank you," said Lockley. And so the three headed for home under a leaden sky, toward the serrated ridge of white cliffs in the distance.

"It surely will be a party to remember," boasted Egbert. "But I'll have to send out new invitations. *No one* would miss a chance to eat Lucy Puffin's fish smidgens!"

On Tytonia, the sun sank below the horizon and cast twilight upon the forest. A small brown bird, a thrush, lit out from her branch, snaring dusk-dwelling insects from the air. Long ago her father had taught her not to leave the Green-Golden Wood of Tytonia, where the songbirds lived, for the nearby swamp known as Slog's Hollow. But the damp ground and humid air of the hollow was home to juicy grubs, beetles, mosquitoes, and fireflies, and the temptation caused many songbirds to stray.

Skirting the edge of the hollow as much as possible, the small thrush satisfied her appetite and began her way home. Crossing a moonlit glade, she glimpsed an apparition out of the corner of her eye that caused her to seize up in terror—an owl. A barn owl, swooping out of the forest on silent white wings toward the middle of the glade. The thrush banked to the left, but the owl did not pursue. It wasn't after her.

She watched the owl dive into the grass and emerge with a rat clutched in its talons. But no sooner had the owl captured its prey than it dropped the rat suddenly, and flew quickly back into the woods.

Curiosity got the better of the thrush. She flew into the glade to examine the owl's abandoned dinner. The rat was alive—but barely. Its black eyes were clouded by a milky film, its fur was mangy, and a blackened tongue lolled grossly out of its mouth. The thrush recoiled in horror at the diseased rodent. The very air around it seemed foul.

She flew quickly away, but in the wrong direction, and by the time she detected the damp air of the hollow and tried to reverse course, it was too late. A blow knocked her to the ground, and before she could right herself, a small but sharp pair of talons grasped her around the throat.

"Don't eat me!" she cried.

A tawny-colored pygmy owl, no bigger than a grapefruit, pinned the thrush to the ground. He stared at her with fierce yellow eyes the size of sand dollars, impossibly large eyes for his tiny head, it seemed. Framing those immense eyes were bushy white eyebrow markings that made him appear as cross as he sounded.

"Why on earth not?" said the owl.

The thrush squirmed in the owl's grasp, searching for a good reason. "I might be sick," she said at last. "Diseased."

"What are you talking about?" said the owl. But the thrush felt his grip loosen. She had struck a nerve.

"Back there, in the glade," she said. "I'll show you." And she took him to the rat, who had since died. But the telltale signs of disease were still there. "If you don't believe me, ask the barn owl I saw try to eat it."

"Another owl saw this?" snapped her attacker.

The thrush bobbed her head nervously.

"Have you seen more like this?" said the owl.

"N-no," stammered the thrush. It occurred to her that

she probably should have lied. If the rat was an isolated case, the owl might not worry about the thrush being contaminated and eat her anyway. But after staring at her for a few more agonizing seconds, the owl released her.

"Spread the word about the rat," he hissed. "But don't dare tell anyone Rozbell let you live."

"Rozbell?" gasped the thrush. But the owl had already flown away.

THE GREAT AUK AND THE LITTLEST OWL

That night, Lockley Puffin dreamt of owls. In this dream, dusk was falling, and at first he only heard them. Their soft hooting seemed to come from miles away. But he walked just a few steps before a lush forest appeared, and from the lowest branches owls were looking down on him, their shapes blurred by shadows but their eyes sharp, unblinking.

Lockley was afraid. His feet were cold. He was standing on ice, he realized, and a chill wind disturbed his feathers. It didn't make sense. There was no ice in the forest. And Lockley's home had no trees—or owls. He looked up again. The trees were now upside down, their gangly roots a cluster of nerves.

No, not upside down. Their leaves had all fallen, and

what he had thought were roots were just bare branches. But in those branches an even stranger sight—instead of owls sitting in their nests, the owls' nests were sitting on them.

Lockley rubbed his feet together . . . they were so cold. . . .

The next thing Lockley knew, he was awake. He was lying on his back and, peering over his round belly, he noticed his orange feet sticking out from under the blanket.

"For the love of fish," he grumbled, trying to pull part of the blanket back from his wife, Lucy, still sleeping soundly. She had become a much heavier sleeper since becoming pregnant, in addition to needing a greater share of blanket, Lockley noticed.

He rolled out of his cozy, down-filled nest, shuffled off to the kitchen to make himself a cup of tea, plopped down in his favorite chair, and promptly fell asleep again. He awoke what seemed like a short time later to the unmistakable smell of slightly burnt fish. "Ah, I bet I know what that is!"

"It's fish!" said Ruby, appearing from nowhere and scaring Lockley half to death. "You can smell it a mile away!"

Lucy Puffin appeared from the kitchen, waddling even more than usual. She carried a steaming tray of what would look to you like tiny crab cakes.

"Who wants a fresh smidgen?" she said.

"I do, I do!" cried Ruby, and before anyone could stop her, she flicked her tongue out and tasted one. "Ugh," she said, recoiling from the pan. "I forgot I don't eat fish."

"Can I have the one she just licked?" said Lockley.

"You overslept, dear," Lucy replied.

"What? What time is it?" Lockley drew back the seal-skin front door and let out a high-pitched scream when he saw a giant whiskered face blocking his doorway.

"Do I smell smidgens?" said Egbert.

Lockley and Lucy had a good-sized burrow, but it certainly wasn't big enough for a walrus. Egbert was often surprising them this way.

"Would you like to try one, Egbert?" said Lucy, offering up the tray.

Egbert studied them carefully, his great whiskers twitching. "No really, I shouldn't," he said. "I'm watching my figure."

"That must take all day," said Ruby.

Ignoring Ruby, he considered the tray a bit longer. "Come outside so I can take a better look." Lucy took the tray outside, followed by the others.

"Oh my, you browned them just right," said Egbert, practically drooling. "Maybe just one." He picked up a tiny smidgen, gave it another sniff, and then placed it gently into his mouth. "Mmm, yes. Flavorful. Tender. Practically melts in your mouth. I must say, quite delicious indeed."

Lucy smiled, but before anyone could move, Egbert grabbed the tray from her and began shoveling smidgens into his mouth. "So good!" he cried, bits of fish flying everywhere.

"Egbert, no! They're for the party!" said Lockley. They tried to pry the tray away from him, and Ruby pulled at his whiskers. The damage, though, was done.

"Well," said Lucy, "at least they were delicious, right?"

"That's why you can't invite a walrus to tea," said Ruby. (Which is probably a sensible rule of thumb to follow even today.)

"You're welcome to tea anytime," Lucy assured Egbert, who was horribly embarrassed. "Now everybody, shoo! I need to get back to work."

Lockley herded his friends toward the water, where he saw a trio of neighborhood pifflings, along with several young murres and guillemots. He smiled. "Boys and girls! Egbert's looking for playmates!"

"Lockley!" cried Egbert, but it was too late—the children were headed his way, squeaking with mischief.

"Let's play Pin the Sea Urchin on the Walrus!" said Arne Puffin, to much agreement.

"I hate that game!" said Egbert, already trying to make his escape. "I always have to be the walrus!" And off he went, scrunching through the sand like some gigantic earthworm, chased by several immature auks and one immature hummingbird.

"That should hold them for a while," said Lockley,

walking back into the kitchen. He reached for a smidgen that had just come out of the oven, but Lucy swatted his wing.

"What's the matter with you?" she said.

"I'm hungry!"

"That's not what I mean, Lockley. You tossed about last night like you were in a sea storm. I woke up without a blanket!"

Not likely, he thought. But what he said was, "Sorry, dear."

She came over to him and rubbed her bill against his. "I know this has something to do with the Great Auk. He's sent someone looking for you twice. Which means you didn't go the first time."

She was right. Yesterday the Great Auk had sent word to Lockley that he needed to speak with him about a vision—a vision of owls. (It was never a good thing on Neversink when owls came up.) Now Egbert had invited owls to his party, and owls were invading Lockley's dreams. He hoped it was just a coincidence, but either way, he didn't want to worry Lucy. "It's nothing, dear. I'll talk to him after the party."

Lucy grunted. "You should be an ostrich if you're just going to stick your head in the ground at the first sign of trouble."

"That's an old wives' tale," said Lockley. "At the first

sign of trouble, ostriches flee."

She stuck a pungent-smelling bag under his wing. "Take these to the Great Auk."

"Were you planning to tell me about this?" said Rozbell.

The small owl with the angry eyebrows pointed to the dead rat as he spoke. In front of him stood the barn owl spied by the thrush, his legs trembling. On either side of the pygmy owl loomed a pair of radiant snowy owls.

"Of course," said the barn owl, his voice quavering. He had good reason to be afraid. For despite being one of the smallest owls in the world, Rozbell was the leader of the opposition party in Parliament and the second most powerful owl on Tytonia. "You—or the Great Gray Owl, of course."

At the mention of the king's name, Rozbell's eyebrows plunged like daggers. "I thought I made it clear that all incidents of this nature were to be reported to me. How many times does an owl in my position have to repeat himself?"

Suddenly, Rozbell began blinking spastically and shaking violently. The snowy owls shifted their feet. Rozbell turned his back on them, and then, over his shoulder, he shooed the barn owl away. The terrified creature left the glade as quickly as possible.

Finally regaining his composure, Rozbell turned to the larger snowy owl and said, "Astra, how many is that?"

"A half dozen perhaps," she replied. "A couple of rats, some small birds. Unless my brother has a different assessment?"

Rozbell turned to the other snowy owl. "Well, Oopik?"

"I haven't seen that many," he said flatly. "But if Astra says so, I believe her."

Rozbell hopped around the ground, churning leaves like a robin foraging for worms. "And what if the Sickness has returned?"

"The entire owl food supply could be threatened, if not the food supply for all Tytonia," said Astra, seeming to dread the thought.

"I don't mean that," said Rozbell. "I mean, what would the Great Gray Owl do?"

The snowy owls exchanged looks before Oopik spoke. "He is one of the few owls to have lived through the last Sickness," he said.

"He didn't just live through it, he ruled during it," snapped Rozbell.

"Yes, and the histories are mixed, at best, on his leadership during that terrible time," said Oopik. "He would be reluctant to acknowledge a new plague."

"Exactly," said Rozbell, fluttering his wings. "His fear is to our advantage. He won't act unless he has no other choice."

"In the king's defense, there is no evidence at this point

that the Sickness is widespread, if it has returned," said Oopik.

Rozbell spun toward him. "It's not the place of *my* second-in-command to defend the king, now is it?"

"My brother only meant, we have time to plan," said Astra, cutting a look at Oopik. "The question is whether there is currently enough evidence of the Sickness to make the king's supporters wonder. We could wait, and hope evidence of the Sickness grows. But if these are isolated cases, then waiting would be a mistake."

"Yes, timing is everything, isn't it?" said Rozbell, but he seemed to be talking to himself as he wandered around in small circles. He had been so close to the throne for so long . . . if the Sickness had returned—or at least, if enough owls *thought* it had returned—he might finally have the chance to prove that the Great Gray Owl was no longer fit to lead them. The king that had let those despicable auks out from under owl rule.

"Just look at this!" sputtered Rozbell, pulling a small scroll of parchment from under his wings. He unrolled it to show Astra and Oopik an invitation to Egbert's party. At the top it said, *You're Invited!* At the bottom it was signed, *Egbert of Neversink.* In between were many, many words, including the generous command, *Invite Your Illiterate Friends Too!* "I found this in my nest. The auks are having a party to celebrate a tooth-walker's birthday!"

"Why would any creature want to celebrate the aging

process?" said Oopik.

"That's not the point!" said Rozbell. "The point is, here we are, faced with the return of a plague that could destroy our food supply, and the auks are *celebrating*! It must be nice to have food that practically swims up to your nest! Am I the only one bothered by this?" He seemed to address the question to both snowy owls, but his huge yellow eyes were fixed on Oopik.

"No one loathes fish-eaters more than I," said Oopik calmly. "If you remember, Astra's and my grandsire was one of the original Roundheads."

"Then you know it disgraces all the owls who came before us to have let Neversink grow more and more independent," said Rozbell. Oopik nodded. "Then you agree with your sister that it's time to act."

Oopik looked at Astra and then at Rozbell. "Parliament normally meets but once a moon. I know you are eager to make your case."

"That doesn't sound like an endorsement," said Rozbell, his voice hardening. Astra looked at Oopik again as if to say, *Tread carefully.* Day was breaking, and Rozbell was eager to sleep. "I've made my decision," he said. "Oopik, fetch that jelly-legged barn owl and bring him to me. He's going to testify before Parliament, whether he wants to or not. And both of you, spread the word. The Roundheads are returning."

The law-speaker's cave was at the southern end of Auk's Landing, a fair distance away. Lockley often thought that was one thing he and the Great Auk had in common—the need to get away. After his flight down the coastline, Lockley alighted, clumsily of course, on the rough shore and wound his way through a maze of rocks to the Great Auk's nest. As usual, the law-speaker was sitting perfectly still with his eyes closed, his body turned toward the sea. The Great Auk wasn't a puffin or a guillemot or a razorbill or a murre. He was, well, a great auk. The primal form of auk. He was the familiar black-and-white, with a long, vertically striped bill like the razorbill. His slender wings were for warmth and swimming only. Like all great auks, he couldn't fly, which was why he lived at sea level.

Closing his eyes was hardly necessary—the old bird was almost blind anyway. But shutting them was his way of inviting the visions he was famous for. Without moving, the Great Auk said, in a deep, growling voice that sounded both stern and wise, "I was expecting you."

"Really?" said Lockley. "You foresaw this?"

"No," said the Great Auk. "I could smell those smidgens halfway up the shore."

"Oh, right." Lockley had almost forgotten them. "Lucy sends her best."

The Great Auk sniffed deeply and then opened his eyes,

smiling. "I should think these would go well with some tea, hmm?"

Lockley sat down while they waited for the tea to steep. Within seconds after they set out the smidgens, the gray sky was a riot of white birds—gulls, terns, and other scavengers—squawking over the fish morsels. They wouldn't dare dive on the Great Auk, Lockley knew. Not out of fear, but out of respect. The Great Auk, after all, had personally negotiated the Peace of Yore with the Great Gray Owl, which let the auks colonize Neversink. And in the years since, Auk's Landing had become a favored stopping ground for migrating seabirds such as arctic terns and black-footed albatrosses.

Lockley always waited for the Great Auk to speak first, in part because he was afraid of saying the wrong thing. Eventually, as he handed Lockley a cup of tea, the Great Auk asked, "Do you think the party will be a success?"

"I'm not sure," said Lockley. "Egbert's quite good at the buildup, but leaves a bit to be desired on the follow-through."

The Great Auk chuckled. "I understand he's promised the colony something that will dramatically change their lives for the better?"

"Yes, can you imagine?" said Lockley. "We fish, we breed, we take tea with our families. How could one possibly improve on that?"

"Hmm." The Great Auk took a loud sip before making a surprising admission: "I've been speaking to Egbert."

"You have?"

"He wants me to tell him the history of Neversink, so he can write it down."

"Is he bothering you?" said Lockley. "I could have a talk with him. Believe me, I have to do it all the time."

The Great Auk set his cup and saucer down with a clatter, which startled Lockley. "I wish the birds were as curious about the history of Neversink as Egbert," he said wistfully. "Or about anything."

Lockley was unsure how to respond. It was highly unusual for anyone but Egbert to say something nice about Egbert. "It's not that. It's just . . . you know everything. You *are* the history of Neversink."

"It may seem like I will live forever, Lockley, but I won't. I am concerned about losing the Stories. Fewer auks are bothering to learn them. They are not mere entertainment, you know. I have long feared they may not be there the next time we need them."

It was hard to argue the point. The generation since the Cod Wars had been so peaceful, most auks viewed the Stories as nothing more than occasional entertainment. "I gather this has something to do with your recent vision?" said Lockley.

"I thought you must have forgotten about that," the

Great Auk said tartly. "I have summoned you twice, after all." For the first time, the Great Auk turned his gaze from the sea and looked at Lockley, his eyes still bright with intelligence despite his age. Lockley felt his neck feathers rise. The raucous cries of circling gulls seemed to be scolding him.

"I've been so preoccupied with Lucy," said Lockley, fumbling with excuses, "and Egbert's party. . . ."

Turning back toward the sea, the Great Auk said, "It wasn't just a vision of owls. It was a vision of owls wearing hats."

"Well, that sounds peculiar," said Lockley. "Why would an owl wear a hat? Also . . . what is a hat, exactly?"

The Great Auk sighed as he gazed in the direction of Tytonia. "A perfect example," he muttered. "When the waters gave forth Neversink, it was a blessing."

"Ah yes, 'The Age of Settlement,'" said Lockley solemnly. Of all the Stories, that was the one everyone knew. At least, they knew the title.

"Indeed," said the Great Auk. "But time has washed away the story's rough edges. There were owls who thought the Great Gray Owl was too permissive—that the auks, having lost the Cod Wars, shouldn't get their own private island out of it."

Lockley couldn't imagine that an owl had anything to complain about. Owls made the rules. For that matter, why had there even been Cod Wars? Owls didn't eat cod!

"Those owls," continued the Great Auk, "so that they could tell who was on their side, began fashioning ornaments for their heads. *Hats.* First out of old nests; later spinning more elaborate pieces from the threads of silkworms. They called themselves Roundheads."

Lockley suddenly thought of his strange dream, with the owls' nests sitting on them instead of the other way around, and a shiver ran through him. "And you fear this faction has returned?"

"I'm not sure they ever really left," said the Great Auk.

"Oh, well then," said Lockley, who thought to himself, *What's all the fuss?* (Which could have been another auk motto.) "I was wondering—did you know Egbert invited the owls? Perhaps your vision was nothing more than a premonition of an exceptionally bad party."

"Possibly," said the Great Auk. "And I don't think there's much to worry about as long as the Great Gray Owl is king. But . . ."

"Yes . . . but?"

"Things change, Lockley. No one rules forever."

Lockley felt another shiver go through him. As he looked back across the sea, the twin peaks of Tytonia seemed somehow closer, larger.

3

THE PLOT IN THE PARLIAMENT

The Parliament of Owls met in a stand of trees that surrounded a small glade. The trees where the members perched, called the Branches of Parliament, curved around the glade in both directions from the king's perch, in the shape of an open talon. To the king's right sat his own party, the Strix. To his left sat the opposition party, nameless since the near civil war among the owls after the Cod Wars.

There are a couple of things you should know about the Parliament. First, because of owls' nocturnal habits, it meets at night, when other woodland creatures are asleep or being eaten by owls. Second, there is generally a great deal of hooting when Parliament is in session. Both general owl hooting, as well as the kind of hooting you associate with ridicule and criticism, since the two parties never agree on anything.

On this particular night, however, there was more murmur than hooting. A general sense of unease could be felt along the branches . . . shuffling feet and tightly clenched talons. The owls knew why this session had been called—word travels quickly through the air, and even the rumor of a Sickness was enough to cause fear in the forest.

The two parties were already perched, and it was the custom for the opposition leader to arrive next, followed by the king. Rozbell's arrival alone was enough to agitate the level of hooting. But after he had flitted in, what he did next caused utter bedlam. He lowered his head and fitted it with a small black hat. And once he had done so, the members of his party did the same. Stiff, short-brimmed black hats with round crowns that fit neatly on top of the owls' round heads. Today you might call them bowlers or derby hats.

The hooting reached such deafening levels that woodland creatures for miles around were sent scurrying for cover. This went on for several minutes, and then abruptly stopped when a booming *whoo-hoo-hoo* echoed through the trees, followed by the *whoosh* of large wingbeats. The Great Gray Owl, king of Tytonia, took his perch.

Rozbell suddenly seemed diminished in the presence of this formidable owl—three feet tall and thick as a boar, with a broad, round face like an orangutan's. He was as gray as the dusk, striped lengthwise, with concentric circles radiating from his yellow eyes. Under his beak were two broad white patches like a bushy mustache. He was now older than anyone could remember, and his health was rumored to be poor. But his revered mind was still considered sharp, and there wasn't a chipmunk, squirrel, or vole in the forest that didn't fear him at the hunting hour.

"Your Majesty," said Rozbell, his voice unsteady. "We are honored by your arrival."

The Great Gray Owl said nothing at first as he looked at Rozbell, and slowly scanned the branches of hat-wearing owls. He then let out a single, deep *whoo* that nearly blew Rozbell off his perch.

"I never thought I'd have to give this speech again," said the king, "but the Branches of Parliament symbolize the World Tree—a World Tree properly dominated by owls. And there were no owls wearing hats in the World Tree!"

The king's party hooted with enthusiasm. But as he waited for the clamor to die down, Rozbell regained his resolve. "No one respects our origins more than I. But we believe the opposition party has gone nameless for too long." Rozbell turned to face the Strix. "Your Majesty should appreciate that for generations, eared owls were considered superior species. Our first half dozen kings were great horned owls or eagle owls. The Roundheads devised the hat to unite us in our causes. They were a sign of equality. And it is a sign of equality for *both* parties of Parliament to have proper names."

It was the opposition party's turn to cheer. From her perch above and behind Rozbell, Astra scanned the faces of the king's party, trying to detect any sign of approval for what Rozbell said. It couldn't hurt to have a few more supporters.

"Those hats have nothing to do with equality," said the king, his voice calm but his tone severe. "We all know why we're here. But I want you to hear it from me—there is no hard evidence the Sickness has returned."

"Here, here!" cried a Strix, and the sentiment spread. But Rozbell was quick to interrupt.

"You'll notice, he said no *hard evidence.* He doesn't have the gizzard to admit we have every reason to fear the worst." Again the Parliament erupted, both sides this time, and the Great Gray Owl began snapping his beak. But Rozbell wasn't finished. "And the reason he won't admit it is, he knows he's powerless to help us if the Sickness has returned!"

The king's beak began opening and closing, but if he was saying anything, no one could hear him over the torrent of hoots. Finally, a scops owl named Otus, the Strix Party leader in Parliament, flew down to a large stone table in the center of the glade. He clutched a rock in his talon and began clapping it against the stone until the Parliament came to order. "May I remind the members," said Otus, "that while we favor spirited discussion, we also favor civility. And we do have rules."

"My apologies to the rule-keeper," said Rozbell, but he tipped his hat as he said so, nearly causing another outcry. "I've seen it for myself, and so have others. Dead rats, mice, and squirrels, all with mangy fur and eyes clouded with death. Songbirds and jays dead on the ground from no apparent cause. We must act now before the whole food supply is contaminated."

"You must think I'm as blind as I am old," said the king, provoking some low laughter. "Nothing in these woods escapes my attention. But death is the natural conclusion of life, even death by disease. You would have us flying into a tizzy at the sight of a bug on the ground."

Rozbell's eyes flashed with humiliation as the king's party snickered. "Your own supporters know you're in denial!" And Rozbell motioned for Astra to bring forward the barn owl, who perched on the stone next to Otus.

"Virgil?" said the king.

Virgil looked at the Great Gray Owl. "It's true, Your Majesty. I recently captured a diseased rat." He glanced at Rozbell. "And I have been in fear ever since."

The barn owl's testimony caused a commotion among the Strix. The Great Gray Owl was enraged. "I was here at the time of the last Sickness," he reminded them. "How dare you suggest I am unable or unwilling to detect such a danger to my subjects."

"That's the real problem, isn't it?" Rozbell snapped. "You *were* here during the Sickness of Yore, and half the owl population was infected or starved to death! *Gewh, gewh, gewh!*"

The hooting surged again, drowning out the sound of Otus beating the rock against the stone. The Great Gray Owl arched his imposing wingspan, trying to intimidate his much smaller opponent. "And I suppose you could just conjure an entirely new food supply out of thin air—*if* the Sickness were to return?"

Astra looked down at Rozbell, who said nothing at first, causing the king to relax his feathers. But Rozbell was merely waiting for the noise to die down before declaring, "In fact, that is exactly what I would do."

The king spun his head left and right as he picked up on a murmur of approval for Rozbell.

"The colony of Neversink has an ample food supply," said Rozbell. "The auks have more fish to catch than a pelican could carry."

The king felt the advantage shift back to him as derisive laughter trickled through the Parliament. "No self-respecting owl eats fish," said the Great Gray Owl. "Except you," he added, pointing to a fish owl, who bowed graciously. "Besides, how would you propose we catch our food? None of us are fishers. Again, except you."

"Not at all," the fish owl replied, bowing with an even greater flourish.

"Who says we would have to learn how to fish?" spat Rozbell. "The auks are expert fishers!"

Otus, the rule-keeper, almost fell off his table, but the Great Gray Owl remained calm. As if he had been expecting Rozbell to wander this way. "And that's the real reason you raise the specter of the Sickness," he boomed. "You're not concerned about our safety in the least." Turning to the entire Parliament, he added, "He and his party are simply looking for an excuse to nurse an old grudge against the auks, and impose their will on the colony."

Hoots of agreement from the king's party collided with hoots of derision from Rozbell's, shaking the trees. "Are you willing to take that risk?" said Rozbell to the king's supporters. "What if you're wrong?"

This time, Astra was certain she could see doubt clouding the faces of many of the Strix. *No one knows how to use fear as a motivator quite like Rozbell*, she thought. The king appeared to see the same thing; the feathers on his neck and head were standing on end.

Otus came to the king's rescue. "Ordering any bird on Neversink to serve us that way would be a violation of the Peace of Yore," he reminded them. "For that matter, so would trying to fish their waters without their permission."

"*Gewh, gewh, gewh!*" said Rozbell. "The Peace of Yore, the Peace of Yore. As far as I'm concerned, it's just something the Birds of Yore talk about. I say, the colonies exist for *our* benefit, not their own."

The Great Gray Owl fired back. "The benefit of letting the auks colonize Neversink was to get rid of those fish-eaters! Stinking up Murre Mountain with their fish and fish carcasses, making enough noise to wake the dead! Aside from that, you all know well the ancient conflict between owls and auks, going back to the World Tree. The situation became untenable. That means it didn't work," he said, sneering at Rozbell. "Getting rid of them *is* the benefit of their being a colony!"

Rozbell, to his dismay, could see the Great Gray Owl regaining command. It was a talent he had through years of practice. Rozbell turned to Astra, who passed him two scrolls. When the hoots of approval died down among the Strix, Rozbell held up the invitation to Egbert's party and said, "I found this in my nest. I imagine many of you did, but you ignored it. You ignore solutions like you do problems!"

"What is that?" barked the king. He directed one of his house sparrows to fetch the scroll and bring it to him. He scanned it, sighing occasionally at the excessive wordiness, then looked at Rozbell. "Some tooth-walker is having a party? That's what you consider a solution?" He let out a great hoot of derision.

"No," said Rozbell. "I consider that a loophole. I consider *this* a possible solution." He passed the second scroll to the king while having Astra distribute several others among the Strix. It was Egbert's revised invitation, promising anyone who attended the chance to try Lucy Puffin's famously delicious fish smidgens. *Life changing! Mouthwatering!* it said. *Puts fish in a whole new light! (And in a delicious crunchy shell!)*

Rozbell turned to address the king's supporters directly.

"If the Sickness is upon us, Auk's Landing could feed us all. And what's more, there may be an alternative to eating raw fish. I am taking a small band to this party. . . . Any of you interested in protecting our future rather than wallowing in our past are welcome to join us."

The king blustered objections amid the uproar caused by Rozbell's offer and looked to Otus for legal aid, but the scops owl quietly shook his head.

Rozbell, feeling he had sufficiently stirred the anthill, said nothing more and led the Roundheads out of Parliament before it was even officially adjourned.

Rozbell met up with Astra and Oopik again, this time in his owlery.

"You made a compelling case," said Astra. "I could see it on the faces of many of the king's owls."

"Yes, well, thank you for bringing me that second

message," said Rozbell. "Those worthless carrier pigeons must have forgotten to deliver mine."

Oopik looked at Rozbell's nest, where an unopened scroll lay partially crumpled, as if it had been sat on.

"I should have known those fish-eaters were bound to eat something other than live sand eels—and *plain* scones, of course." Rozbell laughed heartily at the memory of the decree he had helped push through Parliament. He could barely contain his enthusiasm, cocking his tail and flicking it from side to side. If he could convince more owls that the auks offered a *desirable* food source, he might have feathered his case enough to sway the king's weakest supporters.

"Astra, my pet, you've done well," said Rozbell, glancing at Oopik as he said this. "Now I have to meet someone. Begin putting together the landing party for Neversink." And off he went, undulating toward the forest.

"Well played," said Oopik.

"I'm trying to keep Rozbell happy," said Astra. "You should do the same."

Oopik seemed surprised. "What do you mean, sister?"

"You say what you think too much," said Astra, "instead of what he wants to hear."

"Don't worry, Rozbell needs *both* of us," Oopik assured her. "After all, we are twins. One that has become two. We go together like darkness and light. Even, dare I say it, like owls and hats." As he said this, he pulled off his bowler and kicked it away with contempt.

Astra just shook her head. "You're a fool."

"You don't care about crushing some little island of auks any more than I do," said Oopik.

"No, but I don't care about saving them, either. And I don't want to be on the wrong side of another owl civil war."

"As if we had a choice," said Oopik. "Mother and Father hated the king."

"There you go again," said Astra, "stating unnecessary truths."

Oopik returned his hat to his head. "I will support Rozbell, but I won't bow to him. This is still a parliamentary system, if I am not mistaken. A king is not a dictator."

And with that, the two snowy owls left the owlery, flying off in opposite directions.

THE WORST PARTY EVER (UNLESS YOU'RE A WALRUS)

On the morning of Egbert's party, Auk's Landing was at full throat with anticipation. The air hummed with high-pitched whistles and hoarse growls from the razorbills and murres. Guillemots were wheezing and hissing at everyone. Seals were barking and gulls were scolding. Every burrow, hole, and ledge as far as you could see was occupied by black-and-white birds, some waddling along the rocks, others flying to and from the sea and often landing on top of each other, which provoked even more hissing and growling.

On top of all that, the shore was awash with creatures from Tytonia—at least, ones that could fly or swim: perching birds of many species; giant beavers; river otters. Even among this strange collection of beasts and birds, it was easy to spot the Great Auk. He was at least twice as large as any other auk—more than three feet tall—and when Lockley saw his head bobbing above the sea of creatures, he hurried to catch up with him.

"Oh, hello, Lockley. Quite a turnout, no?"

"I have to admit," said Lockley, "I have no idea how Egbert managed to draw this sort of crowd."

"He's a resourceful one, to be sure," said the Great Auk.

"Especially when it involves himself being the center of attention," said Lockley.

They both chuckled and walked on until they were in sight of the Thermals, where the party was to be held. "I need to go meditate before my presentation," said the Great Auk.

"Of course," said Lockley.

But the Great Auk didn't leave. "I assumed you caught up to me because there was something on your mind?"

"Oh, right," said Lockley, embarrassed that he was still so timid around the law-speaker. "I was just thinking . . . perhaps, based on our previous conversation . . . perhaps it would benefit all of us to hear a story about how we came to be here. You know . . . who we are, and why our way of life is worth preserving."

The Great Auk looked kindly at Lockley. "We'll speak again after the party."

The Thermals were great, boiling fountains of water called geysers that sprang forth from the earth. Their periodic eruptions created warm, steamy air and permanent hot springs, which the auks found soothing. It was clear that many guests had come to see the great towers of white steam—and to visit the Guillemots' Bazaar, a sort of marketplace where creatures could exchange goods and services. These included spa services: preening (for the feathered) and cleaning (for the furry); talon or claw sharpening; paw-pad buffing; tail fluffing; bill polishing; deep-tissue massage; and parasite and insect removal.

The bazaar was run by a crusty old guillemot named Algard. Because of his expertise, Egbert had asked him to help organize his "surprise" birthday party—even though Algard failed to understand the point of celebrating the aging process. At the moment, Egbert was hovering over the guillemot's every move, appearing to offer helpful suggestions. Algard appeared not to be appreciating Egbert's advice. Though it was hard to tell—guillemots always look a bit sour. Unlike puffins and razorbills, they have narrow bills that taper to a point, as if they're permanently pursing their lips at you.

There were also arts and crafts for sale. (Or trade, to be more accurate. At this point in history there was no such thing as money, because only marsupials had pockets.) Ivory and wood sculptures. Decorative skin rugs or wall hangings. Feather-down pillows and blankets. All in all, there was much to do other than acknowledge Egbert's birthday, which is exactly how Algard had planned it.

Lockley let out a deep sigh: "No owls." Relieved, even pleasantly surprised, he wandered around the bazaar until Lucy arrived. He helped her set up her smidgens station, and though he would never admit it, he was proud that his wife's treats had much to do with the large crowd. Lucy would never show off, of course. But Lockley was happy to do it for her. *Why do puffins always have to be so humble?* he thought. Eventually he followed the crowd to an open, grassy area, where a large flat stone sat in the middle of the Thermals. He and the others formed a semicircle on the scrub grass around the stone and waited.

Before long, the Great Auk appeared through clouds of hot mist and walked slowly toward the stone platform. He kept his small wings clasped behind his back, the way people with a philosophical bent often do. As he took his place atop the stone, geysers erupted in turns behind him. The effect was something like a statue in a plaza fountain.

No one was sure exactly how old the Great Auk was. In the time before the time of humans, animals of all kinds lived much longer than they do now. Perhaps because they didn't keep track of every second of every day, so that they weren't constantly worrying about "where all the time went." There was little doubt, though, that the Great Auk had lived in the Days of Yore (which, as best this author can tell, was what birds called any period of history that most of them couldn't personally remember).

Traditionally, he appeared before the colony for two reasons: to Speak the Histories and to Speak the Law. Auks were not as highly organized as owls. Families generally dealt with their own problems. But if disputes could not be settled, the Great Auk was summoned by the Council of Elders to judge who was right and wrong under the law. As law-speaker, he had also represented the auks before the Parliament of Owls.

On more ceremonial occasions, the Great Auk assumed the role of history-speaker, in which he told the auks one of the great stories of their past. "The Cod Wars" and "The Age of Settlement." "The Betrayal of Alca Torda." "The King of Murre Mountain" and "The Island of the White Seal." At least, those were the titles Lockley could recall now, watching the Great Auk wait for the auks and their visitors to fall silent.

"I've thought a great deal about which story I want to tell you," said the Great Auk. He stretched himself to his impressive full height, to better project his voice. "I think I should tell you again of the World Tree. And afterward, I think there are some treats we are all looking forward to."

All heads turned in the direction of Lucy Puffin. Off to

the side, a dejected Martha Razorbill stared at her unpopular caramel snails.

"As some have heard told," said the Great Auk, "the First Goddess gave birth to the world in the form of an egg. And day and night she protected the world-egg from harm. But in the regions of darkness lay coiled a giant serpent, who plotted to take the egg by trickery and devour it.

"One day he came to the First Goddess in disguise, and told her about a nest of vipers nearby that wished to destroy her egg. He warned her to seek out the nest and crush the vipers while they slept. And in this way he tricked the First Goddess into leaving her egg.

"The giant serpent captured the egg in his mouth and tore it apart with his fangs. When the First Goddess realized she had been tricked, she flew into a rage and called all the gods to war against the serpent. They finally slew him, but it was too late to save the world-egg. In mourning, they planted a seed in the blood that grew into the World Tree, which branched into the Past, Present, and Future. And they created the perching birds to carry time through the branches, and the oceans to nourish its roots, and the Eagle to protect it."

There was a murmur of appreciation among the crowd as they pictured the towering strength of the World Tree, listened to the far-off currents of the sea washing against their shores, and admired the Eagle's courage.

"It was in the Past that the Birds of the Four Talents roosted," the Great Auk continued. "The Merlin, the Auk, the Raven, and the Owl. Each had one gift to bestow upon the other birds. The Merlin gave the gift of flight. The Auk gave the gift of swimming. The Raven gave language. And the Owl gave wisdom—but only to other owls, which destroyed the harmony that once existed among all birds."

Many auks softly clicked their bills at this reminder of the owls' betrayal.

"The Auk demanded that the owls be punished for their selfishness. But the Merlin and the Raven refused because the four birds roosted equally in the World Tree. The Auk took away the gift of swimming from owls, ravens, and merlins. The Merlin and the Raven retaliated, taking back their gifts from the auks. In protest, the Auk left the World Tree, and no auk has roosted in a tree since."

The Great Auk paused and looked at the faces in the crowd, as if to make sure they all appreciated the significance of this.

"From the World Tree the first Great Auk led us to Murre Mountain"—and here the Great Auk gestured across the ocean, in the direction of Tytonia—"where he learned the gifts of language and wisdom on his own, and shared them with other auks. He even learned the gift of flight in order to teach it, though he himself never practiced it. And Murre Mountain is where we would be to this day, if not for the owls."

Everyone nodded in agreement, in defiance almost, at the mention of owls and the suggestion of what had gone before.

"We should all be proud of what it means to be an auk—simple in our ways and self-reliant, born with an innate sense of justice and a love of community. Never take your blessings, most of all your independence, for granted. Now, before we go and enjoy the rest of our celebration, I think we should take a moment to give thanks to Sedna."

A remarkable quiet fell over the large crowd as the auks silently gave thanks to the goddess of the sea, who controlled all the beasts and fishes of the ocean and provided the rich harvest of Neversink's waters. She was known to be a vengeful goddess, easily offended. And she had a complicated history with the birds. The auks were ever mindful of this. After a few moments the Great Auk lifted his bill to sniff the briny air, then turned and came down from the stone.

"Marvelous," said Egbert, who had somehow managed to sneak up on Lockley. "Such a wonderful story, 'The World Tree,' and such a durable element of bird mythology."

"Mythology?" said Lockley.

"Oh, certainly," said Egbert. "Talk to the great migrators

and you'll find there are similar stories all over the known world. Each one tailored to a given territory. A perfect example: near the Southern Ocean the auk is replaced by a penguin."

A penguin in a tree. Lockley had never heard of anything so silly. Egbert, though, was eager to begin his big presentation. He lumbered off toward the rock where the Great Auk had just spoken. Ruby was already there, Lockley noticed, busy covering something with a small grass mat, tugging at the corners with her tiny bill.

"If I can have everyone's attention, please!" Egbert shouted above the din of birds. Most of them thought there would be a feasting period between speeches, and they were quite disappointed to learn otherwise. "Everyone, please, look this way!"

Egbert had now raised up his enormous, wrinkled body until he looked like a giant termite mound. But when everyone did finally turn in his direction, all they saw was the dark flock of birds soaring through the white steam of the Thermals, descending slowly on the island.

As the birds neared, it became obvious that they weren't a flock. They were a parliament. Owls had arrived on Neversink: a pair of snowy owls, swan-white and shrieking as they extended their feathered feet for landing; a pair of splotchy brown hawk owls, letting out a piercing *kwikikikik-kik* as they swooped low over the tundra; a barking, brown eagle owl, even larger than the snowy owls.

There were others, which Lockley thought might be long-eared owls or great horned owls. But it was impossible to tell. For these particular owls were all wearing hats. They began perching wherever they could, even on top of stunned auks. And finally, fluttering to the front like a moth compared to his larger companions, was a small, tawny owl wearing a small black hat. The entire colony of auks was rendered speechless by the invaders and their alien headgear. Fear and confusion seemed to paralyze everyone, except Egbert.

"Rozbell!" he exclaimed. "What an honor! I never dreamt someone of *your* stature would come."

"Yeah," said Ruby, appearing over his shoulder. "We weren't expecting anything smaller than a shrew."

Rozbell's enormous eyes seemed to expand even further to take in the entirety of the walrus. "You must be that *tooth-walker* I hear so much about."

Egbert bristled. "My good sir, you probably aren't aware that *tooth-walker* is an offensive term. Nevertheless, I'm delighted you received my invitation!"

At this, the colony erupted in a chorus of angry bird noises. Lockley wanted to use the chaos to sneak away. After all, he had defended Egbert when he first proposed the party. He had even convinced Algard to help Egbert out. Lockley caught Algard's eye; the guillemot, as if reading

Lockley's mind, opened his black bill and stuck out his red tongue at Lockley.

"Yes, your invitation," said Rozbell. He produced the small scroll and had Astra deliver it to the Great Auk, who was the only auk not to seem surprised by all this. "Not that I need an invitation to investigate unauthorized assemblies in the territory," Rozbell added, with a decided emphasis on the word *unauthorized*.

The pygmy owl flitted over to Egbert's makeshift podium. "What's *this*?" he snapped. And to Egbert's horror, Rozbell clutched the grass mat in his talons and stripped it away, revealing . . . *something*.

Egbert let out a sigh that was like a gust of wind. "It's a book."

"What in the name of the World Tree is a *book*?"

"I was building to that," said Egbert. At which point he launched into a lengthy monologue on the genius of the walrus mind, the expanse of the walrus imagination, and the invention of writing by walruses by carving slabs of ice with their tusks—exactly the sort of thing you should be grateful I omitted from this version of the story.

Finally getting to the point, Egbert began flipping the pages of his book as he explained, "Many pages of parchment can be folded up and stitched together like so and printed front and back, so there's virtually no limit to the number of words I, *er*, any author can use!"

A guillemot standing at the front said, "You do realize that none of us can read or write?"

"Not *yet*," said Egbert.

"He's invented a printed version of himself," said a razorbill. "Big, heavy, and it just goes on and on and on."

Many of the auks and even a few of the owls wearing hats laughed, but Rozbell just stared in disbelief at Egbert. He hopped right onto Egbert's book, his legs straddling the spine, until he was beak-to-snout with the walrus. "*This* is why you called the whole territory together?"

Egbert clapped his fins to his face, genuinely surprised by Rozbell's hostility. "I thought you and your friends above all would be interested in this," he said. "After all, most owls *can* read and write. And owls are legendary for their gift of wisdom, although I think we all know that's just a myth. I must admit, however, that your binocular vision does give you a certain bookish quality. But the brain in a creature your size couldn't be any larger than a walnut. . . ."

"Silence!" screamed Rozbell. "Doesn't he ever stop talking?"

Everyone just shrugged.

Rozbell was so angry he began panting. He could feel his eyelids twitch. *Not now*, he thought, and he pulled the brim of his hat lower on his face as he twitched and flinched, and his fellow owls began arching their wings and shuffling nervously from one foot to the other.

As the tension built, Lockley frantically searched the crowd for Lucy. If he could find her, maybe he could sneak her away from the gathering before something terrible happened. He began to pick his way through the look-alike birds when he noticed the tall head of the Great Auk shrinking from view. Surely their leader wasn't sneaking off—not when they really needed him!

Lockley needn't have worried, though. At this moment, Rozbell wanted nothing more than to leave the island immediately, before losing control in front of everyone, especially the fish-eaters. And he might have (no one will ever know for sure) if another of Egbert's annoying tendencies hadn't come into play—his desire to impress everyone.

Seeing that Rozbell was going to order the other owls to take flight, Egbert blurted out, "Don't leave yet!" Raising himself up, he spotted Lucy near the back. "Not without trying one of Lucy Puffin's fish smidgens!"

Suddenly, Rozbell stopped blinking, and a calm came over him. Of course, the reason they came . . . "Smidgens?"

At that moment, Lockley regretted that he'd ever encouraged Egbert to stay on Neversink.

"Oh my, yes," said Egbert, parting the sea of birds as he lunged forward. "Follow me." He led Rozbell and the others over to Lucy's booth. To her credit, she stood her ground as the menacing group of strangely clad owls came toward her.

"What, exactly, is a smidgen?" said Rozbell, picking up one of the small morsels for a better look. He placed the smidgen in his beak and begin to chew. Fishy and yet *not* fishy. The juices mixed with the crunchy bread crumbs and the seasonings. . . . Rozbell felt his mouth water.

Yes, his mouth watered! Like a common fish-eater! They didn't *look* like fish. That was a point in their favor. And the taste! Rozbell's eyes blazed with excitement as he realized the tooth-walker had solved all his problems. Here was a delicious alternative to eating raw fish—the bait he needed to win more owls to his side. He greedily grabbed the remaining smidgens and began passing them out to his followers.

Lockley forgot to breathe as he watched this bizarre scene. The Great Auk couldn't have foreseen this: Owls With Hats savoring his wife's special dish. He didn't know what it all meant, but he was sure it couldn't be good.

MURTHER MOST FOWL

Every culture searches for ways to describe the falling of darkness, with all its mystery and shades of symbolism. Dusk. The gloaming. The hour of the bat. In the bird world, they know it as the time of the owls.

Neversink experienced the white night of summer, the constant light of a sun that barely set from June to August. But on Tytonia darkness fell. The time of the owls came.

On this particular night, dusk fell on a night with a waxing moon. Rozbell came awake, his lower eyelids descending. Astra and Oopik, both day hunters, arrived just as Rozbell finished tucking a small bundle into the crown of his hat and returned the hat to his head. He traced the stiff, black brim with his foot, admiring the fit.

"How do I look?" he said. The snowy owls clicked their beaks, and Rozbell flew off from Slog's Hollow, the grim swamp he called home.

Between Falcon Crest and Murre Mountain, Tytonia dipped into low-lying hills and swamps blanketed with a dense, velvety forest known as the Midland Woods. Here the Great Gray Owl lived in a thicket of shrubs and small pine, spruce, and tamarack trees in an area known as the Green-Golden Wood, for the way sunlight spattered against the leaves in the afternoon.

The pygmy owl flitted into the king's lair as quietly as a sparrow. There was a stillness; the owlery was empty—almost. Rozbell noticed that the ground was covered with half a dozen cages made of twigs and vines, most containing various small animals, all still alive. Before he could look more closely, the booming *whoo-hoo-hoo* of the Great Gray Owl echoed through the trees, and the king landed on a branch across from Rozbell.

Pretending not to notice his visitor, he dropped a struggling chipmunk into one of the empty cages. He then opened another, snapped up a squirrel, and swallowed his wriggling prey with several horrible gulps.

"I see that His Majesty continues to ignore the peril of eating infected food," said Rozbell.

"I ignore nothing in this forest," the king growled. "Each of these cages represents a different capture day. The squirrel I just ate was captured five days ago. I believe it reasonable to expect that he would have exhibited signs of disease in that time if he were infected. So not only am I ensuring the safety of my own diet, I am performing an experiment of sorts. Thus far, no animal I have captured in the past week has proven to be diseased, which argues strongly against the return of the Sickness."

Rozbell arched his eyebrows at this. "Well, your system is certainly preferable to becoming a *vegetarian*," he said.

The barb caused the king to snap his beak. According to the histories, the Great Gray Owl had ordered all owls to stop hunting live prey during the last Sickness. The result was that birds of prey had to suffer the shame of picking seeds and berries like common finches.

"I'm surprised you have the nerve to come in here without your pets," said the king.

"Astra and Oopik provide needed security," said Rozbell.

"I never needed a bodyguard."

"You were . . . are . . . large and fierce, Your Majesty. I am but a humble pygmy owl."

"Humble?" The king let out a high-pitched hoot. "Leadership isn't about physical power, unless you're one of the toothy beasts of the ground."

But as he said this, the Great Gray Owl arched his imposing wingspan and flew to the branch next to Rozbell, emphasizing the difference in their sizes. He leaned forward as if examining a particularly icky bug. Rozbell could feel the king's breath on his face. The feathers on his head and neck began to stand.

And then, Rozbell blinked. Literally. A series of rapid, uncontrolled blinks, as if someone had just squeezed a lemon in his face. He tried to control himself, but the sting of humiliation only made it worse.

The Great Gray Owl watched this spasm of blinking and let out a series of great hoots. "Ah yes, there it is," said the king with smug satisfaction. "That pathetic lack of self-control that keeps you in your place. You're a great agitator, Rozbell. You've proven useful many times. But you are no leader."

The king let fly several more hoots and shook out his wings. He was in full gloat. But he had been in power for so long, his authority unchallenged for ages, that he made a considerable mistake: he underestimated his small foe. Staring with contempt at the bowler on Rozbell's head, he said, "And one more thing. This is *my* owlery. *No hats!*"

He swung his right leg out, kicking Rozbell's hat squarely on the brim and sending it flying behind him. As the hat flew off, a small bundle fell to the ground. "What is that?" said the king.

Rozbell's blinking subsided and his feathers relaxed. Hopping over to the bundle and unwrapping it, he showed the king two small brown clumps that smelled faintly of burnt fish. "These, Your Majesty, are called smidgens."

The king looked closer. "What is a *smidgen*?"

Rozbell smiled. "Smidgens are the reason my plan *will* succeed." The pygmy owl examined both smidgens, then carefully placed one in his beak, savoring the tender, cooked flesh as it melted in his mouth.

"Give me that!" the king said as he snatched the other smidgen from Rozbell. He held it up to his beak and sniffed it. "You went to Neversink, to that party! After I ordered you not to!"

"I guess some things *do* escape your attention," said Rozbell.

The king popped the smidgen into his mouth. Rozbell watched as his face registered the same surprise, the same amazement at the mixture of flavors, the same disbelief that he was eating a lump of fish. Then the king's eyes widened and his wings drooped. He tried spitting out what he hadn't swallowed, but it was too late.

"Don't worry. The pain won't last long," said Rozbell as the king collapsed to the ground. "I think the lesson we've all learned here today is that dangerous things sometimes come in small packages."

The Great Gray Owl stretched his wings as if to take off, but the poison had disoriented him. He struggled to keep his balance.

"Not that you'd get very far," said Rozbell, "but I can't

risk your leaving the owlery."

Just as the king wobbled to his feet, a phantom plunged through the trees and struck him to the ground. An immense bird of prey, speckled white with a hood of brown feathers, seized the king by the wings with his cruel talons. He lifted him up and threw him down again at Rozbell's feet. The bird greedily eyed the king's throat, but a look from Rozbell stayed the attack.

"I'd like you to meet the newest member of my team," said Rozbell. "This is Feathertop. Have you ever seen a larger bird of prey?" Rozbell looked admiringly at the martial eagle, a native of Africa, who had one stray feather that stuck out from the back of his head.

"They'll know it was you," gasped the king.

"Sadly, Your Majesty, forensic science at the present time is appallingly crude. No, others will come in here and see that you took your own bad advice, continued to eat live prey, and fell victim to the very Sickness you insisted on denying. Killed by your own arrogance. Thanks to you, my case will be even stronger."

Rozbell returned the black hat to his head and stood over the fallen owl. "Oh, I know what you're thinking. Never in too much pain to look down on me, to lecture me on how fear is a poor motivator in the long run. Continue frothing at the mouth if you agree—good.

"Now, let's be honest. Don't pretend for a minute that

you didn't use fear, didn't use your size to bully smaller owls. Hawk owls, great horned owls, *snowy* owls—you *all* do it. For all our supposed learning, has there ever been a pygmy owl or a screech owl king? Of course not! *Gewh, gewh, gewh!*

"*I'm no leader?* Not only have I brought the Roundheads back, but our numbers are greater than ever—thanks to those smidgens. The *nonpoisonous* kind, of course."

Rozbell laughed maniacally, his tail bouncing up and down. "If only our old-fashioned system of government allowed us to vote you out of office, I wouldn't have had to kill you. *Thank heavens* for our old-fashioned system of government!"

Rozbell's eyes seared with hatred. He gave the Great Gray Owl no chance to respond, for by the time he was done ranting, the king was dead.

Otus had just returned from a hunt when Astra and Oopik swooped down on either side of him, framing the bark-brown owl in white.

"I thought the king's owls feared no Sickness," said Oopik, noticing the half-eaten earthworm in Otus's beak. The elderly scops owl wiggled his head as he swallowed the rest of his catch. The pale feathers under his neck had grown loose with age, like a graying beard.

"I am no longer agile enough to snare insects and bats," he croaked. "What do you want?"

"Call Parliament into session," said Astra.

Otus's narrow ear tufts stood up straight. "Why?"

"Because the Great Gray Owl has died," said Oopik, clicking his tongue in annoyance. "And because Rozbell said so. Enjoy your last act as rule-keeper."

Any creature within hooting distance of the Midland Woods that night could have told you this was no ordinary session of Parliament. The king's lifeless body lay upon the stone table, a sight that caused mournful calls from the branches of the Great Gray Owl's supporters. And then, the former king's party members were forced to remove themselves to the other side of the glade, while owls wearing hats—the Roundheads—took their perches along the honored right-hand branches.

From his perch, Otus declared, "We have a long tradition in Parliament, that a king, once chosen, rules as long as the gods allow. When that king passes to the spirit world, though, we duly elect a new king. Allowing all members of Parliament a voice prevents any one party from . . . *abusing* power." Otus nearly choked on his own words and had to pause. Like most of the king's former party, he knew the election had been a sham; few would dare to defy Rozbell now. "Members of Parliament," he continued, his voice wavering, "the votes have been tallied. May I present your new king."

The new opposition party, now nameless, seemed to have lost their voices as well, perhaps stunned by the sight of the hat-wearing pygmy owl fluttering through the branches to take the king's perch. Roundheads hooted with glee, and once the noise died down, Otus held out his stone gavel to Rozbell. "It is your first privilege to choose a new rule-keeper," said the scops owl.

Oopik arched his wings. He and Astra were the new king's top advisers, and he was the male, after all. But Rozbell, after glancing at Oopik, turned to Astra instead. "Astra, trusted descendant of the original Roundheads, will you honor me by vowing to keep our rules and protect order?"

Astra hesitated briefly, but Oopik nudged her with his wing. She glided down to Otus's perch and took the stone gavel from him.

"Very good," said Rozbell. "And now, despite our heavy hearts and sour gizzards, we must carry on. The loss of a king as great and as long-serving as the Great Gray Owl cannot be overstated. But I would argue that his death is proof that it was time to move on. As you all know, the king refused to admit that the Sickness might be upon us again. And he died eating contaminated food."

Rozbell took perverse satisfaction in the fact that what he said was, technically, true. His eyes darted around the Parliament until they landed on Otus. Otus had flown directly to the king's owlery after his visit from Astra and Oopik. Sure enough, he found the Great Gray Owl on his back, dead, along with Rozbell and his monstrous new companion, Feathertop. Rozbell had explained that they'd found the king this way, and he had pointed out the frothing around the king's mouth. But Otus had noted the lack of milky eyes typical of the Sickness, and he had noted also the signs of struggle.

Otus lowered his eyes, and Rozbell went on: "Whether the Sickness has returned in force or not, I'm sure you agree it is vital that we have a solution, if worse comes to worst. I alone have provided a solution."

The opposition party began hooting nervously as they realized what Rozbell was building to.

"The colony of Neversink has a plentiful food supply, and a plentiful workforce to collect enough food for all of us," said Rozbell. "Furthermore, as those of you know who made the trip to Neversink with me, the auks have a desirable alternative to eating raw fish."

As his supporters whistled, Rozbell had a basket of smidgens brought forth and distributed among the Parliament. Some of the opposition refused to eat, but others nibbled at the smidgens, and their faces betrayed a sense of pleasure. Rozbell smiled.

"I hereby propose, therefore, a tax on the fish caught daily by the auks of Neversink. And that the taxed portion be turned into fish smidgens for the owls' consumption." The hooting once again reached earsplitting levels, but Rozbell raised his wings to quiet supporters and dissenters alike. He stared off through the trees, into the darkness, his bright eyes aglow. "And in order for this new decree to take effect, I hereby declare the Peace of Yore to be officially *dissolved*."

There was one other order of business on that fateful night. Rozbell arranged for the Great Gray Owl to be given an official burial, according to parliamentary tradition.

You might be fooled into thinking Rozbell was attempting to show the former king respect. In fact, he knew that many suspected the Great Gray Owl did *not* die of natural causes. But by observing this ritual, Rozbell was continuing the illusion of a legitimate change in power. It made it that much harder for his opponents, who already feared him, to question his authority.

The Ceremony of Farewell, as it was called, took place two days later. It required placing the dead king on a bed of branches from his own owlery, then pushing him off toward Ocean's End, until he disappeared over the horizon to a resting place beyond the known world.

From this resting place, the spirit of the fallen leader could return should his territory ever need him again. The Great Gray Owl himself was thought by some elders to have been the reincarnation of Tytonia's first king, Longshanks, who had ruled as the Great Horned Owl.

"What a crock," Rozbell said to himself as the ceremony took place. But he wasn't about to take any chances.

Once the raft had slipped over the horizon and Parliament returned to the Midland Woods, Feathertop took flight out to sea. He caught up to the slow-floating funeral barge and savagely carved up the corpse with his tenterhook of a beak, until the once mighty owl looked like a mutilated feather bed. The eagle then capsized the raft, sending what was left of the body to a grave at the bottom of the sea. There would be no heroic return by the spirit of this former king to save Tytonia.

PART TWO
Over Sea, Under Ground

THE FISH TAX

Word of the Great Gray Owl's death gathered over the territory like thunderheads. Even before Rozbell's decree was officially delivered to Neversink, pelicans, terns, and gulls had broadcast the news, igniting a great coastal howl among the colony. Rozbell ruled the land.

It was perhaps fitting that Lockley had been at home, trying to find enjoyment in a plain, dry scone, when he heard the news. Lucy was resting, still exhausted from all her work for Egbert's party, and Lockley thought it best not to disturb her. But when he went to check on her, she was sitting up in the bed, worrying the blankets with her wing tips.

"I guess you heard, too," he said. "Why do gulls have to be so noisy?"

She shook her head, clenching the blankets. "What are we going to do, Lockley?"

He couldn't think of anything comforting to say, except, "Perhaps it won't be as bad as all that."

She looked up at him, and he came over to the bed and hugged her next to him. "If we have to make a few extra smidgens, I'll help. You'll see."

The decree, once officially delivered, confirmed their fears: the fish tax, the smidgens. . . . But auks are creatures of habit. (All creatures are, really, but auks had elevated habit to an art form.) And despite their uproar at the news, most took few pains to obey the new tax. Some would take their leftovers, if they had any, to Lockley and Lucy's door. But the truth was, Lockley himself could catch most of the fish necessary for all the smidgens Lucy could comfortably bake in one day.

Unfortunately, this wasn't nearly enough to feed all the owls of Parliament, to say nothing of all the owls of Tytonia. (Although, to be fair, Rozbell only cared about pleasing the members of Parliament—the owls with clout.) In fact, the first few batches weren't enough to satisfy Rozbell alone.

"Where are the rest?" Rozbell's voice reverberated off the walls of his owlery, his beak stuffed with smidgens. It had been a week since the initiation of the fish tax, and he had taken to shoving three or four in his mouth at one time, so that Astra and Oopik could barely understand him.

Leaning in closer to hear better just meant getting sprayed with bits of fish and bread crumbs.

"These are all the puffin has made," Astra explained. "It would appear that many in the colony are being . . . *complacent* about the new decree."

Rozbell inhaled the rest of his mouthful. "Complacent? *Complacent!* Wait—that means they're not doing it, right?"

"Yes, Your Majesty."

"*Gewh, gewh, gewh!* You see what the Great Gray Owl allowed to happen?" The agitated pygmy owl flitted over to Astra. "Your grandsire, Olaf, would never have tolerated a colony of auks thinking they didn't have to obey us. What is the World Tree coming to?"

The king seemed on the verge of a breakdown when Oopik interjected, "Perhaps a reminder?" Rozbell spun his gaze over his shoulder, as if he'd forgotten Astra's brother was there. "Make an example of some bird. Remind them where they belong in the pecking order."

Rozbell's tail dropped slightly and his eyelids lowered. "Hmm. I like that idea. Of course, it means another trip to that frozen rock they call a home, but so be it. *Feathertop!*"

The martial eagle pulled his beak out of the mangled remains of some small mammal.

"Time to introduce yourself to Auk's Landing," said Rozbell. And then, much to the surprise of both snowy owls, Feathertop dropped to the ground and bowed his head, allowing Rozbell to climb onto the back of his neck like a tick. Apparently using his own wings for such a long flight was now beneath him. The king grabbed the eagle's neck feathers and looked at Astra and Oopik. "Are you two coming?"

If the auks of Neversink thought they would never see anything more disturbing than an invasion of owls wearing hats, they were wrong. Algard Guillemot, who was in the middle of griping to Lockley about some minor offense, was among the first to see the martial eagle, ridden by the king of Tytonia, descending on the island, flanked by Astra and Oopik. Before long the shore and the sea cliffs were a chatter of nerves. The colony watched Feathertop alight on a large rock at the foot of the cliffs and stoop to let Rozbell dismount.

"Lucy, go to the bedroom," said Lockley.

"What's wrong?"

"I'm not sure. Just please, keep out of sight."

Lockley returned to Algard's side as an odd hush fell over the normally chaotic colony. Rozbell basked in the disturbance he had caused for several moments before he spoke.

"There was a time when decrees issued by the Parliament of Owls were taken seriously," he said, drawing out his words. "Apparently times have changed." He let his words seep in, like the tide to the sand. "Or perhaps the Great Auk failed to tell you about the fish tax?" There was a low hum of nervous energy all along the cliffs. "Where is your fearless leader, by the way? Is he here?"

Lockley wondered the same thing. And where were Ruby and Egbert? Just when a distraction might be welcome, the five-thousand-pound walrus was nowhere to be seen.

"Let me explain to you how a tax works," said Rozbell. He nodded to Feathertop, who hopped off the rock they were perched on and began stalking through the agitated crowd. "You catch a certain number of fish a day. The tax requires you to submit a portion of that to me. Or to the smidgen cooker, what's-her-name." He quickly glanced around, but puffins all looked alike to him.

One auk after another stiffened with fear as Feathertop walked slowly by, stabbing his talons inches from their webbed feet, flexing his seven-foot-wide wingspan, and clicking his hooked beak with menace.

"It's a percentage thing," Rozbell added. "Not unlike a game of chance." And with that the king hopped down off the rock and scratched around in the sand until he came upon a pebble he could grasp. "Catch," he yelled as he tossed the pebble high into the air in the direction of a group of auks.

An unlucky murre, reacting on instinct, not wanting

to be hit in the head, caught the rock as it fell toward him. There was a frozen silence, and then Feathertop launched himself at the poor bird, snatching him up by the shoulders and carrying him to Rozbell.

The eagle opened and closed his beak near the terrified murre's neck; Lockley couldn't look and turned away. "Astra and Oopik will remain here," said Rozbell, "in case anyone else has questions about the fish tax." He ordered Feathertop to lower his head so he could remount. And then the eagle took flight, carrying the hopeless murre off with them.

In the weeks that followed, migrating birds might have been forgiven for thinking that Neversink had become an ant farm. Coasting high above the island and looking down on a given day, they would have seen hundreds of small, dark creatures marching across the rocks and along the shore in an orderly, continuous, single-file procession. The line would meander toward a certain spot, where each creature, in turn, deposited something into a pile. At which point they would double back, the line unbroken and unhalting, in large part because of the two white creatures who appeared to be marshaling this unusual parade.

Rozbell's cruel lottery had had a chilling effect on the colony. Fish were piling up faster than Lucy could use them. And she was baking day and night, hoping to make sure Rozbell had his daily fill, if nothing else. But there was no way she could feed an entire parliament of owls, and she prayed to Sedna that other owls would be too afraid to complain to the king if they weren't getting their share.

The lottery had had a chilling effect on Astra and Oopik's relationship as well. For one thing, Rozbell had made them governors of Neversink, to enforce the fish tax and to remind the auks that owls could now be anywhere he wanted them to be. Snowy owls normally inhabit wintry climates, but neither Oopik nor Astra wanted to live among a colony of auks. Astra blamed Oopik for this.

"It was your suggestion to make an example of one," she said as they watched this day's procession of auks paying their tax.

"You're the one who said I should keep Rozbell happy," Oopik replied coolly.

"Higher creatures shouldn't exercise their power without a purpose," said Astra.

"And taking that bird hostage didn't serve a purpose?" As if to demonstrate, Oopik launched himself from the boulder they were standing on and lunged at a slow-moving puffin, barking at the terrified bird. The line began to move faster.

"That's not what I meant," said Astra. "The appearance of that eagle alone would have had the same effect. And stationing us here was to punish you for defying Rozbell earlier."

"Then why are *you* here?" said Oopik. "He likes you, *rule-keeper.*"

"Owls are superstitious," she replied, ignoring the jab. "He's not sure what would happen if he physically divided us."

"Well, I have a feeling your duties as governor will far outweigh those of rule-keeper," said Oopik. "I doubt much will be up for debate in Parliament anymore."

Astra said nothing as she watched the endless line of auks, coming and going.

Lockley emerged from his burrow, carrying a bundle in each wing and one in his bill. He waddled under his burden down an algae-covered slope to the shore, where he dropped the bundles on a pile already there, awaiting pickup by a squadron of pelicans. He took the long way back home, trying to avoid his fellow colonists as much as possible. Many blamed him for all this, and Lockley halfway agreed with them. He never should have been boastful about Lucy's smidgens. Maybe he did support Egbert's party because he wanted to show Lucy off. Well, he had certainly gotten plenty of attention, for the both of them.

Lockley was so preoccupied with his own grumbling that he walked right by the kitchen and almost didn't notice Lucy. She was squatting down on the kitchen floor with her wings dunked in a bucket of cold water.

"What's the matter?" said Lockley, and as he pulled her up, he saw that the tips of her wings were nearly bare. The feathers were singed from going in and out of the oven so much.

Lockley felt his concern turning to anger. The tax was a burden for the entire colony. But sacrificing a part of your daily catch was one thing. Everyone shared in that. Cooking smidgens, on the other hand, fell to one bird only—Lucy Puffin, whose legs had already been beginning to strain under her pregnant weight even before the tax. Before having to cook smidgens day and night, for fear of being the next bird Rozbell decided to make an example of.

Yes, he was angry at Rozbell. Angry at owls in general. Even angry at Egbert, his friend, who had brought him so much grief. But he was angry at auks, too, and their way of doing things. Auks prided themselves on their self-reliance and tried never to burden others with their troubles. Which presented Lockley with a problem. Lucy couldn't possibly cook all those smidgens on her own. He wouldn't allow it. But the proper thing to do was to suffer in silence. *That's the Aukward way*, he reminded himself.

"There's only one thing to do," he said, still holding Lucy's bare wing tips in his own. "I'll have to ask the Great Auk."

"Ask the Great Auk what?" said Lucy.

"Ask him to make the whole colony chip in on the

cooking," said Lockley. "You can teach the others. If it comes from him—"

"No!" cried Lucy. "That wouldn't be right."

"Lucy, they're already angry with me. You know, Rozbell didn't have a chance to try Martha Razorbill's caramel snails. . . ."

"Lockley! How could you even think of doing that to Martha!"

"Because I can't stand what this is doing to you!" he snapped.

Lucy came closer to him and rubbed her broad bill against his. "I know you mean well, dear. But Rozbell . . . you can imagine what he's doing to that poor murre. Who knows what he's capable of? We've caused enough trouble for now." She managed a wry smile and added, "Besides, I no longer have to worry about burning my wing tips, since I don't have any. Let's see how it goes and hope for the best." (Which could have been another auk motto: See How It Goes and Hope for the Best.)

The problem was, Lockley had a strange feeling that hoping for the best would be useless, and that you didn't need to be the Great Auk to see where things were going. He thought of making his way to his private ledge—oh, wouldn't this be the perfect time to soar? To leave his troubles far below? But as he looped inland to avoid the remaining taxpayers, he passed a talking boulder. At least, it appeared to be talking. Lockley stopped and listened to the familiar voice.

"Do you think he's still mad at me?" said the walrus.

"Could you be more specific?" the hummingbird replied. "Everyone's mad at you."

"I think he means me," said Lockley, circling the boulder to find that it concealed Egbert (it was a *very* large boulder) and, of course, Ruby.

"Lockley! I was afraid you weren't speaking to me," said Egbert, whose pink face was splotched with worry.

"I'm not mad at you," Lockley lied. "You didn't mean any harm."

Egbert slouched in relief, allowing his flab to expand horizontally. "My dear, you must let me help set things right. I've been preparing an inspirational speech to rally the colony to the cause of resistance!" Up he went again, as if addressing a crowd. "Imagine a moving introduction, followed by passionate exposition, tears, applause, etcetera, concluding with the rousing declaration: Ichthyological Taxation Without Representation Shall Not Stand!"

After a moment of uncomfortable silence, Ruby asked, "Is *rousing* another word for *boring*?"

"I'm afraid that may have too many syllables to be a good rallying cry, old fruit," said Lockley.

Egbert became defensive. "I suppose you can do better?"

"I'm not sure," said Lockley. "What exactly did all that mean?"

"Well, it's quite clear, really," said Egbert. "It decries the essential lack of fairness in a governmental system in which the ruling party, in this case, the Parliament of Owls, enforces rules upon a governed party, in this case auks, without giving said governed party an opportunity to debate the enactment of said rules in the aforementioned Parliament." When neither Lockley nor Ruby appeared to understand anything he had just said, Egbert sighed and added, "Essentially, *No more fish tax.*"

"Why didn't you just say that?" said Ruby, tweaking Egbert on the forehead.

"Ow! All those words can be found in this book," Egbert retorted, producing a slim volume entitled *Important-Sounding Words for Correspondence, Letters to the Editor, and Political Rallies.* "It's written by a leading authority on the subject."

"It's written by you," said Lockley.

"Precisely. I suppose I could dumb it down a little, if you insist. Back at my nest I have a new book I'm working on that helps you find words that are similar to other words. I call it the *Walsaurus.*"

"Egbert!" said Lockley, trying to hide his irritation. "I don't think the colony is quite in the frame of mind for a revolt just now." Lockley doubted whether any of the auks he knew would *ever* be of a mind to revolt. Certainly not after Rozbell's display. But seeing how disappointed Egbert was, Lockley felt bad for his friend. He really did mean well.

Suddenly, Lockley hit upon an idea. "Egbert, do you really want to help?"

"Of course, my dear!"

"Me too!" said Ruby.

"Good," said Lockley. "Come with me."

"Where are you taking me?" said Lucy.

"It's a surprise," said Lockley.

"I have smidgens to make!"

"Exactly," and he led her through a maze of rocks to a clearing where Egbert, Ruby, and Arne Puffin and three of his friends stood next to a pile of fish and a long, flat stone.

"What's going on?" said Lucy.

"Meet your new assistants," said Lockley.

"Wait," said Snorri Guillemot. "Is this a chore?"

Leave it to a young guillemot to be disagreeable, thought Lockley. "No, I told you, it's a new game you get to play with Egbert." When the children looked at him skeptically, he added, "You get to pulverize stuff."

The children cheered as Lockley moved everyone into position and said, "Watch this, dear."

Egbert, Lockley, and the four young auks attacked the

pile of fish with their bills and small rocks, chopping, dicing, and mincing the fish into ground meat. Next, they all sprinkled various ingredients into the ground fish, and then Egbert rolled lengthwise along the stone, like a colossal rolling pin, mashing everything together. Then the team went at it again, separating the mixture into small clumps. And finally, Ruby buzzed down the line, sprinkling bread crumbs on top of the raw smidgens.

"See? All you have to do now is put them in the oven," said Lockley.

Lucy clicked her bill with pleasure and grabbed the first new batch of ready-to-bake smidgens. "Thank you all," she said. "You are good eggs."

"I'm going to walk her home and then be back with more ingredients," said Lockley. "We don't want to stop while we've got Egbert on a roll!"

The children squeaked with pleasure again as Lockley and Lucy walked off. He put his wing around her, and he allowed himself to feel proud of his own cleverness.

A SMIDGEN TOO FAR

No one was more pleased by Lockley's new production process than Rozbell. His appetite seemed to have no bottom, and the pygmy owl had gone from the size of a grapefruit to more of a ripe cantaloupe in just a few weeks. Meanwhile, other owls were receiving the same small allotment of smidgens, and some began to suspect Rozbell was taking more than his fair share.

"How dare they!" said Rozbell, to no one in particular. Feathertop sat filing his beak on a large branch while house sparrows and an elderly short-eared owl busied themselves in various states of servitude. Rozbell was reading a very politely worded request, signed only, *The Parliament,* which suggested that the greater incoming load of smidgens might mean more for all.

Feathertop glanced at the golden-brown hoard piling up under Rozbell's perch.

"It was my idea, after all! Most of them laughed at me!" The king was agitated now, flicking his tail and hopping from branch to branch. As much as he resented their request, he was paranoid about disloyalty. How could he appease them without given up his own surplus?

Suddenly his eyes widened. "More fish means more smidgens!" he said, his tail cocking up and down. "Let's double the tax—no, triple it! Isn't it fun watching the fish-eaters come up with new ways to accommodate us?"

The short-eared servant owl, named Alf, spoke up: "Your Majesty, shall I send word for Astra to return and call Parliament into session?"

"What for?" snapped Rozbell. "Astra and Oopik are the only two owls on Neversink. Just have them *tell* the auks we raised the tax. What's the difference?"

Alf looked at Feathertop, who just shrugged. Rozbell noticed this.

"What? You don't agree?"

"I didn't say anything," stammered the old owl. "Whatever you wish."

"I *wish* everything didn't have to be so *difficult*," griped Rozbell. "Forget the tax. You!" he screeched at a returning pelican, whose throat-pouch puffed out in alarm. "You and your rubber-necked pals, I'm expanding your duties. Get it—*expanding*?" Rozbell filled his cheeks with air as if he had a gullet full of fish, then began laughing hysterically.

Two mornings later, Lockley woke up to find what looked like half the fish in the ocean piled up outside his door. He wondered if he had slept through several days of tax collections, when suddenly a fleshy storm of fish rained down upon him, knocking him to the ground. He looked up at a squadron of pelicans soaring away from him.

"What in the name of Sedna is going on?" he wondered aloud, and then noticing winged shadows swooping over the ground, he looked up just in time to see a second squadron descend and open their mouths, bombing him again with cold fish.

"I think we have a problem," said Lockley, ducking back inside his burrow. Lucy poked her head out of the kitchen.

"What's the matter, dear?"

"I can't believe I'm saying this," said Lockley, "but I think we may need more walruses."

Starting that day, Lockley, Lucy, and the team were so busy making smidgens they barely had time to eat or sleep. The fun of it quickly disappeared for the young birds, and Lockley could hardly force them to work. That left fewer laborers for more smidgens.

To save time, they began using Egbert's avalanche of

a body to smash the raw fish, but the results were disastrous. A typical new batch had entire fish eyeballs or tail fins sticking out, more scales than bread crumbs, and overall the smidgens began to taste more like walrus hide than fish. Even Egbert turned his nose up at them.

"What are we going to do?" said Lucy. "These will never satisfy Rozbell!" Lucy didn't just fear Rozbell's wrath. Her strong sense of pride made her hate the fact that she was churning out a product unworthy of her.

"He's got to have piles of smidgens by now waiting to be eaten, even if he's feeding every owl on Tytonia," said Lockley. "Maybe we have some time before he gets to the wonky batches."

That was small comfort to Lucy, who felt compelled to take over most of the prep work as well as the cooking. Lockley hated to go behind Lucy's back—she had forbidden him to ask the Great Auk for help—but he felt he had no other choice. And so he waited until she was distracted, and then he grabbed one of the remaining good batches of smidgens and quietly left the burrow.

After his wobbly landing, Lockley sploshed across the wet rocks to find that the Great Auk already had tea for two set out. "I gather you heard about Rozbell's visit," said Lockley.

"I saw it," the Great Auk replied. Lockley wasn't sure

if he meant *saw* as in he'd seen it, or *saw* as in he'd dreamt about it.

"Then you must know what's happened since. We—Lucy—can't keep this up. Something has to be done."

"Indeed," said the Great Auk.

"Yes, well that's why I'm here," said Lockley, hesitating. "We all share the fish tax of course, but the real work is Lucy's—making all those smidgens, day after day. If you could see her wing tips . . ."

"And what do you plan on doing about it?" said the Great Auk, turning to Lockley for the first time.

"This, actually," said Lockley. "That is, I thought *you* could help. It would be unseemly, of course, for me to ask the colony to help make the smidgens, in addition to paying their taxes. But if it came from *you* . . ."

The Great Auk seemed to slump a little, and returned his gaze to the sea. "Lockley, what would happen if I did that?"

"Well, as I figure it, we would go from the unfairness of one auk making *all* of the smidgens to all of the auks making *some* of the smidgens, thus easing Lucy's burden and allowing us to regain some normalcy in our lives, outside of the fish tax and the owls and all that."

"I see," said the Great Auk. And then, after a pause: "I have to say, Lockley, I'm very disappointed that your concerns are so small."

Lockley felt the irritation all the way to his underfeathers. "With all due respect, I don't think Lucy's well-being is a small concern at all. You haven't had to watch *your* wife turned into a virtual slave by Rozbell!"

"No, I haven't," said the Great Auk. "But tell me this, Lockley. What happens after I do this? Isn't the fish tax still in force? Aren't the owls still intruding on our lives?"

"I suppose."

"And what does that likely mean?"

Lockley thought about it for a moment, then admitted, "They're owls. And not just any owls. Owls With Hats. Which means they are likely to keep intruding."

The Great Auk nodded. "And what is injustice, even if spread evenly?"

"It's still injustice."

"As you can see, foresight is really just a product of reasoning," said the Great Auk. After a pause he asked, "Do you know why the Cod Wars were fought?"

"Cod, I guess," said Lockley.

The Great Auk sighed deeply as he turned back toward the sea. "Owls don't eat cod," he said, which Lockley had always wondered about. "It was a *tax* on cod."

"There was another fish tax?"

"Yes, for the privilege of using Murre Mountain. Can you imagine? Our ancestral home. Settled by the first Great Auk. And they wanted to *rent* it to us." His voice was filled with disgust. "One of the things I've always liked about you, Lockley, is your appreciation for the Stories. And not just because it flatters an old bird like me to have someone listen to him. The Stories are important."

"I know," said Lockley.

"You *think* you know. The colony can't always rely on me to tell them what's important and what's not . . . what's worth remembering and, most critically, what's worth fighting for."

Then who? thought Lockley.

"If more auks had a passion for our heritage," said the Great Auk, "where we came from and how we got here, they would perhaps be more passionate when a creature like Rozbell threatens to alter their way of life. The wave laps the rock, and the rock does nothing, except erode."

"Yes," said Lockley, who certainly agreed that some of his fellow auks did remarkable impersonations of rocks. "I do think, whatever our failings, we still have enough pride to resist injustice when it confronts us." He wanted to remind the Great Auk that that was why he'd come down here to begin with, but he decided that would be rude.

The Great Auk again looked at Lockley. "Those who fought the Cod Wars were willing to die to live independently of owls. Are *you* to that point yet?"

Lockley was chastened, but also still irritated that the Great Auk thought his concerns were trivial. "Are we really independent? We're still a colony of Tytonia." He couldn't help himself.

Returning his gaze to the sea, the Great Auk said, "Sometimes compromise is necessary. Fanatically embracing any idea, even a noble one, can be dangerous."

"I'm sorry," said Lockley. "I spoke out of turn. We have been independent. We've hardly been aware that owls even exist, much less govern our territory. That's why it's so discomfiting when they do step in, like that whole unpleasantness with the cranberries. And now this. We don't know quite what to do."

"I'm not sure I do either, if that's what you're getting at," said the Great Auk. "I can't tell anyone what they should be willing to sacrifice or for what end. But as for your present concern about Lucy's labors, that may resolve itself."

"What do you mean?" said Lockley.

"Sedna will not tolerate this demand on her generosity," the Great Auk explained. "Rozbell doesn't understand this, for obvious reasons. Meanwhile, the auks invoke Sedna's name as a matter of habit, but I'm not sure they understand the price of gluttony, either." He glanced at Lockley, as if to assess whether he fit this description.

"What's the worst that can happen?" said Lockley.

"The worst that can happen? Not only would there be no fish smidgens, there would be no fish. Period. We would have to migrate to a new territory to find food. And as you know, for any birds that are pregnant, or have laid their eggs or hatched their young, this would be impossible."

"So we would starve."

They finished their tea before the Great Auk spoke again. "Lockley, I need you to understand something. Those times when you've spoken up, as with the cranberry tariff . . . others may have seen you as petulant, but I see in you a willingness to stand up for what you believe is right. Something inside you smells injustice the way you can smell a sand eel, and rebels against it."

"Sand eels?" said Lockley.

"No, Lockley. Injustice."

"Oh yes, of course." Lockley blushed. Or at least he would have, if puffins could blush.

"You're right that the burden of the fish tax is unfairly shared," continued the Great Auk. "But so is the burden of leadership, Lockley. You see what's at stake, even if the rest of the colony can't, or refuses to. And the fact that this is so personal for you gives you the authority to act."

Leadership? Authority? Lockley thought he must have seaweed in his ears. Perhaps Lockley's kindness and curiosity and occasional pluck made him different, but a leader of the colony? A puffin with the title of Great Auk? The mere thought would have sent a laughing gull on a three-day bender.

"Why do you doubt yourself, Lockley?"

"I don't understand what you're asking," Lockley replied. "*You're* still the Great Auk, the law-speaker."

"The Great Gray Owl and I wanted the same thing—distance from each other. I'm afraid Rozbell may have started a chain of events that I don't have the strength to resist."

Before Lockley could protest, the Great Auk said, "There's something I've been meaning to give you." And he held out a sealed clamshell attached to a lanyard. "I have a notion it might prove useful to you at some point."

Lockley took it. "Shall I open it?"

"Open it when you need to," said the Great Auk, and so Lockley placed the clamshell around his neck, tucking it into his breast feathers, hoping very much that he would know when that time was and what to do with whatever it was.

"Consider what's happened so far," said the Great Auk, "and think hard about all that could be lost. Deep down, the colony knows the owls are to be feared. But right now they fear taking action more."

Lockley left the Great Auk realizing that he fit that description as well. Why else would he have flown to the Great Auk for help? He returned to his burrow muttering to himself again (a bad habit of his), and walked right by what he thought was the empty kitchen. But when he went to the bedroom, Lucy wasn't there, either. It wasn't possible she could be out, thought Lockley. She had barely had time to stick her bill through the door for fresh air since the pelicans started raining fish outside.

He walked back to the kitchen, and there was Lucy, slumped on the floor, sobbing quietly, a tray of smidgens upturned on the floor next to her. "Oh dear," said Lockley as he bent to help her up. She pulled her wings away.

"Just leave me here. Leave me alone," she said, barely audible.

Lockley stood back for a moment, looking at Lucy. Except for her belly, every part of her looked thin and worn. He could see the skin at her elbows and wing tips. He felt his gizzard grinding, and he tasted venom on his tongue. He reached for her again and pulled her up. She didn't resist this time. He led her to the bedroom and helped her lie down. "You've made your last smidgen," he said, covering her with blankets. "Rest yourself. I'll be back."

Lockley walked onto his ledge and looked out over the sea. The sun was near its highest point, its bright light making the ocean's surface seem sheer and translucent. Normally at this time of day Lockley could look into the middle distance and see the frosty blue water darkened with ribbons of fish, the colony's lifeblood. But what the Great Auk had warned him of was already apparent—the waters had been overfished; the blood was thinning.

Lockley stood there and thought about the promise he had made to himself to protect Lucy and their egg at all costs. He felt foolish for believing that accommodating the owls would accomplish this. They only wanted more. The problem was, how could he get the rest of the colony to react? Their burden had actually lessened—the snowy owls didn't seem to care whether the auks contributed any more fish to a pile that was already overflowing with pelican catches. So what, in the Great Auk's words, would they be willing to sacrifice to help Lucy and Lockley?

He gazed again into the distance and wondered just what might happen if the fish disappeared. *The worst that could happen is we all starve.* It was a sobering thought. Had he, like his ancestors, reached a point where he was willing to die to live independently of owls? If the Great Auk was right and the overfishing continued, it might not be up to them. Maybe he could get that to sink in with the rest of the colony. If not to help Lucy, perhaps they would act to save their own skins.

It was on this foundation of logic that Lockley built an idea.

"Say that again?" said Egbert, who couldn't believe his ears.

"I said, you were *right*," Lockley repeated.

Ruby buzzed close to his ear. "Are you sure about that? I don't think we want to encourage him."

"I'm sure," said Lockley. "I want to take this to the beaches."

"To the commoners?"

"Why just the common murres?"

"Not common *murres.* Common*ers*," said Egbert. "And I insist you let me help craft your speech. Just because you want to speak *to* the commoners doesn't mean you have to speak *like* them."

"I never called the other auks *commoners*," Lockley asserted.

Egbert sat down and began scribbling feverishly, occasionally putting his quill pen to his lips as if in deep consideration of a brilliant turn of phrase. Finally, he stood up and positioned himself at his full height, and in his most dramatic speaking voice declared the following:

"I, Lockley J. Puffin, despite being a puffin, with all its attendant shortcomings, having taken it upon myself as a plenipotentiary of the island of Neversink, whose heretofore thought-of independence is lately threatened by the usufructuary actions of certain owls, to require that the aforementioned owls both cease and desist such actions, forthwith and posthaste!"

The surrounding area went deathly quiet. Even Ruby sat down. "I think that's a great starting point," said Lockley. "But I may . . . *edit* it a bit."

"Yeah," said Ruby, "like take out all those words no one

knows. Basically everything after 'I, Lockley J. Puffin.'"

Egbert's whiskers bristled. "Fine, *simplify*, if you must." And he slouched off in a huff.

"What are you going to do, Lockley?" said Ruby.

Lockley gazed out across the ocean toward Tytonia, a place to which he felt an ancestral bond though he had never lived there. "We're going to have another party."

"I think Egbert may have given *party* a bad name," said Ruby.

"Just get everybody to the meeting place in a hour," said Lockley. "You'll see."

THE WORST PARTY SINCE CHAPTER 4

Lockley was pacing back and forth, working a rut into the middle of his burrow. Lucy was practically tracing his steps, trying to hand him a cup of tea.

"Lockley, take this right now before it's all sloshed out."

He paused long enough to take a sip.

"I added some lemon and honey, for your voice," said Lucy.

Ruby appeared in the doorway, followed by Egbert, who was brandishing his pen.

"What's that for?" said Lockley.

"I think this rises to the level of an official meeting,"

said Egbert. "You need someone to keep the minutes. For posterity."

"How do you keep minutes?" said Ruby. "And where? In an hour, I suppose, but then where do you keep your hours? And what does your posterior need with them? Is that where you keep everything? Is that why it's so big?"

"That's enough, you two!" said Lucy. "Lockley is under enough stress as it is."

"Thank you, dear."

When he finished his tea, Lucy took the cup from him and then turned him toward the door. "They're all waiting on you," she said. "And we're right behind you."

They rubbed their bills together, and Lockley emerged from his burrow. The whole colony was there, or so it appeared. Hundreds of puffins, guillemots, murres, and razorbills, along with a few curious seals and other seabirds as well. There hadn't been a gathering like this since, well, the birthday party. But before that, it had been a *really* long time since there had been such a gathering.

"Exactly how did you get everyone here?" Lockley asked Ruby.

"I told them the Great Auk called the meeting," she explained. "Let's face it, no one was showing up just to see *you*."

On that inspirational note, Lockley took a deep breath

and walked boldly up to the same high rock where Rozbell had introduced the colony to Feathertop. Astra and Oopik perched above the crowd, betraying no emotion.

Algard Guillemot, naturally, was the first to protest. "Where's the Great Auk?" he asked. Others nodded, wondering the same thing.

"Ruby may have misspoken," said Lockley, his voice unsteady. When murmurs of complaint began to work their way through the crowd, he raised his voice and said, "Can you do nothing for yourselves without the Great Auk's counsel?"

"What is it we're supposed to do, exactly?" said Algard.

"Stand up for yourselves. Not let yourselves be bullied by owls." Lockley pointed in the direction of the formidable snowy owls as he said this. He managed to keep his legs steady, even though the pit of his stomach reminded him of the time Egbert had given him some bad clams.

"Or maybe some of you are grateful to finally have a ruler who takes such an interest in us. Who oversees our every move. Maybe some of you need that kind of attention."

The remark was met with a mixture of nervous laughter and low hissing. Lockley paused and cleared his throat, trying not to lose his confidence. "Rozbell ends the Peace of Yore. Rozbell imposes the fish tax. Rozbell takes one of our own and then leaves snowy owls here to remind us that any one of us could be next. He has you marching in file like penguins, but your response to this erosion of our way of life is to say, *Don't Make Waves!*"

For once Lockley directed a withering look toward Algard, instead of the other way around. The rest of the colony seemed both embarrassed and irritated by Lockley's chiding.

"But I understand," said Lockley. "After all, I am an auk. Moreover, I am a puffin. So I understand as well as anyone that you are all afraid. But I also understand that our ancestors sacrificed much so that we could live independently. Have you already forgotten the Great Auk's message before Egbert's party? That we should all be proud of what it means to be an auk? To not take our blessings for granted? Well, that's exactly what we are doing by letting the owls plunder our waters! Have none of you noticed the dwindling bounty when you take to the sea to fish?"

Many in the crowd looked at one another and quietly nodded.

"This isn't just about fish smidgens or the burden of paying a tax to the owls. This is about respecting ourselves and our way of life! *Don't Make Waves!*" Lockley squawked again. "Well, I say there comes a time when you *have* to make waves!"

The crowd gasped.

"Look at that pile," said Lockley, indicating the mound of fish near his house. "The big lump of evidence that the owls own us. Our stinking pile of shame!"

Egbert, for one, couldn't believe what he was hearing. "He hasn't used a single important-sounding word!" But Ruby shushed him.

"What do you propose we do?" said Algard.

"Here's what I want you to do," said Lockley. "I want each of you to grab a fish and chuck it back into the ocean. To tell the owls that the blessings of our waters are sacred, and not to be pillaged! As of right now, Neversink pays no fish tax to owls—with or without hats!"

No one moved. Not Egbert, not the auks, not even the snowy owls. Astra, for her part, watched with something close to curiosity, it seemed. As if she simply wanted to see what happened next.

Which was this: As the colony of auks just stood there, trying to grasp what they'd been asked to do, Ruby left Egbert's shoulder and buzzed over to the fish pile. She found the smallest fish she could find, a tiny sand eel, pinched it by the tail, and with antlike strength lifted it into the air. The multitude watched in amazement as the hummingbird, sagging with her burden, swerving like a drunken bumblebee, managed to reach the water, whereupon she dropped the fish.

Plunk.

Lockley could scarcely believe it himself. Nor did he truly expect what happened next. Someone let out a scream and ran for the pile, and the next thing he knew, auks were chucking fish back into the sea by the dozens. Not every auk participated, but you couldn't tell that from the roar they made. Even Egbert charged into the fray, colliding headlong with the pile like a flabby locomotive, plowing a huge swath of fish back into the surf.

The fish party continued until the pile was all gone. Only then did an exhausted Lockley and his small band of revolutionaries stop and look at what they had done, and consider who they had done it to.

Astra and Oopik exchanged glances and then flew off silently, leaving the colonists to wonder what their outburst would bring.

That night, Lockley dreamt he was wrestling a prickly puffer fish in freezing cold water. He awoke to find his blanket gone and Ruby poking him in the chest over and over again with her needlelike bill.

"Ruby!" he whispered, trying not to wake Lucy. "What the devil is it?"

"Come outside," she whispered back. "I need to show you something."

As he stumbled through his living room he looked wistfully toward the kitchen. "Do I have time for a cup of tea?"

But Ruby was already through the door.

"What time is it?" Lockley wondered as he stepped outside.

"It's almost dawn," said Ruby. "Or dusk. I can't tell in this crazy place!"

The sun wasn't yet visible, but an amber glow surrounded them, and the placid sea reflected the sky's mixture of gray shadow and soft light. Lockley could barely make out Ruby's iridescent green body winking in the twilight, but he could follow the tremendous hum of her wingbeats as she led him down to the water's edge.

"Ruby, what are we doing?"

"What do you see?" she asked, hovering over the water.

Lockley saw nothing, and said so.

"Where are the fish?" Ruby asked.

"*Under* the water?" Lockley timidly offered, wondering if this was a trick question.

"Actually, I meant that *rhetorically*," said Ruby.

"Rhetorically?"

"It's a word I learned from Egbert. As best I can tell, it's just a way for creatures who love to hear themselves talk to keep talking."

"Ruby . . . ," said Lockley, growing impatient.

"The point is, the fish aren't there!" she said, upturning herself and pointing her bill at the water. "At least, not as many of them."

"What makes you think that?" said Lockley.

"Fur seals."

"Pardon?"

"Fur seals," said Ruby. "They fish mainly at night, and a family I'm friends with complained that the pickings were slim."

"Wait," said Lockley, trying to get a handle on all this while still half asleep. "You're friends with a family of fur seals?"

"Do you think my life revolves around *you*?" Ruby asked.

Lockley was speechless.

"The point is, Lockley, I think something may have happened."

Lockley plunged into the water; he had to see for himself. Across the shallows he went, slowly descending the sloping sides of the volcanic island until he was flying through deeper and deeper water. The first thing he noticed was a surging current of cold water that normally didn't channel this close to the island. He paddled through it, but he was at least fifty feet down before, finally, a small school of sand eels swam by, followed by a trickling of char.

After a half hour's fishing, Lockley returned to the surface and hopped back onto the shore. As he shook off the excess water, he thought to himself, with a mixture of fear and excitement, that his plan just might have worked after all.

"What do you mean, there are no fish?" said Rozbell, with surprising calm. "You've *collected* no fish? The auks have *caught* no fish?"

Oopik looked at Astra. Neither of them wanted to explain. Finally Oopik said, "Actually, Your Majesty, it would appear there are no fish to catch. In the ocean. Period."

"Let me see if I have this straight," said Rozbell, his beak grinding ever so slightly. "In the whole ocean, there are *no fish*? Is that what you're telling me?"

"Not in Neversink's waters, anyway," said Astra.

"How could there be *no fish*?"

Rozbell glanced at his current supply of smidgens, his desire to consume with abandon suddenly conflicting with a desire to conserve. "Maybe it's a trick," he said, his eyelids beginning to twitch. "Their devious way of getting back at me . . . denying me my smidgens . . . mocking our food crisis by creating one of their own." He began hopping from branch to branch now, talking to no one in particular. "No . . . being devious takes brains. No fish-eater is clever enough to think of that."

Oopik let out a short, shrill laugh. "You're right about that, Your Majesty. The puffin and his friends who threw all the fish back into the sea—anyone could have told them such a show of ingratitude would have angered Sedna."

Rozbell alighted on a branch just above Oopik. "Sedna?"

"Their goddess. The provider. A vengeful goddess, as the seabirds tell it."

"And you let them do it," said Rozbell, barely loud enough for anyone other than Oopik to hear.

"I'm sorry?"

Rozbell darted to the other side of the owlery and perched facing the snowy owls. "I made you governors of Neversink to make sure the fish were collected and the smidgens were made! Not to let the auks exercise their rights of assembly and speech! *Gewh, gewh, gewh!*"

His staccato syllables ricocheted off the trees; Rozbell's house sparrows began to flutter. Astra stole a glance at Feathertop, who began baring his tongue at the sound of his master's overheated voice.

Rozbell continued to sputter, and then his saucerlike eyes again fell upon the most recent bundle of smidgens to be delivered to him—the last bundle of smidgens to be delivered to him, if there were no fish to catch. You could see him processing this reality, his bushy white eyebrows jumping up and down. "This is your fault! You let this happen!" he said, turning on Oopik again. "I've never had your full support. Maybe you *wanted* this to happen!"

Astra tried to speak up on her brother's behalf, but he held a wing out to stop her. "Your Majesty, you know that's not true," Oopik said calmly.

"Do I?" said Rozbell. He turned to Feathertop and

uttered a chilling two-word command: "Kill him."

As the eagle stretched his massive wings, Astra spread hers too, a reflex to defend her twin. But it was too late.

Feathertop launched himself at Oopik. The large owl left his perch as well, colliding with the eagle in midair. Astra felt the talons in her chest, the beak at her throat. And as Oopik died, she felt part of her die too. Her stomach churned as she watched Feathertop wipe the blood from his beak.

"Traitors," Rozbell muttered when it was all over. "That's why I brought in Feathertop. Because you can't trust an owl."

Then, to Astra he said, "You and Feathertop. Go and bring me the Great Auk. And while you're at it, fetch the troublemaker as well."

"'The *Something* of Sedna,'" said Lockley. "'The Wooing of Sedna.' 'The Courting of Sedna.' No, that's not it. 'The Splendor of Sedna.' 'The Haunting of Sedna.'" He began to get frustrated. "Fish brains! Why can't I remember?"

In case you were wondering, angering Sedna was not part of Lockley's plan. Perhaps he should have foreseen it. *But after all,* thought Lockley, *I'm not the Great Auk.* He couldn't help feeling some irritation at the old bird for throwing him out of the nest on this one. But now that it had happened, maybe he could use it to his advantage.

That's what had excited him when he confirmed Ruby's

fears. *Even Rozbell can't force you to make fish smidgens if there are no fish.* Maybe the owls would lose interest in Neversink. Then the Great Auk could appease Sedna and restore their food supply. If there was suffering in the short term, it was the auks' own fault.

Appeasing Sedna. Lockley felt he needed to warn the Great Auk of this possibility now that his plan had made a bigger splash than intended. But as he made his way down the coastline, he realized he would seem more prepared if he could remember the formal name of the Sedna story first. For the love of fish, the Great Auk had just been warning Lockley about how the colony was forsaking its own culture!

He had hoped that saying at least part of the name aloud would help him recover it. But so far, no luck: "'The Source of Sedna.' 'The Creation of Sedna.' 'Sedna Under the Sea.' 'Sea for Sedna' . . . well, that one's just ridiculous."

When Lockley arrived at the Great Auk's nest, however, he soon had much bigger concerns. He found the nest empty, with broken tea cups, loose tea leaves, and various other personal items strewn about.

He looked up in time to see what appeared to be the Great Auk, struggling as he was carried off in the talons of what could only be the enormous eagle under Rozbell's command. A high-pitched bark caused him to turn around. The last thing he remembered was a white owl with a rock in its talon, and then everything went black.

CAPTURED!

When Lockley awoke, he found himself suspended from a branch in a cage made of twigs and thorny vines. He was surrounded by trees in a dimly lit grove and could see very little at first. *Where am I?* he thought, and as his eyes began to adjust, he saw the Great Auk suspended in an identical cage nearby. He then remembered the blow to the back of his head and felt the egg-sized lump that was there as a result.

"I guess things didn't work out quite as we planned," said the Great Auk.

He looks even worse than I feel, thought Lockley. *He must have been handled roughly.* "I suppose not. But it is closer to what I expected." Looking around the grove, Lockley asked, "I don't suppose you saw the murre Rozbell took from Neversink?"

The Great Auk shook his head.

There was a rustling among the leaves, and suddenly Lockley was confronted by an enormous pair of yellow eyes as Rozbell perched on one of the crossbars of his cage. The white shadow of Astra floated onto a nearby branch, and the hooded head of Feathertop was just visible in the dusky distance.

"So this is the troublemaker," said Rozbell in his rapid, clipped cadence. "I'll deal with you later," and he snapped his beak at Lockley, causing him to jump backward. Rozbell then flitted over to the Great Auk's cage.

"Well, well, well. If it isn't the law-speaker. The Wise One. The Repository of All Knowledge of Auk Lore. The Aged Leader of Neverstink! Wait, *Never*stink would be a *good* thing. How about *Ever*stink? Yes, that's better!" And Rozbell hooted with laughter.

"Why don't you just call me Great Auk?"

"I'll call you whatever I want," said Rozbell, his laughter dissipating in a fog of rage. "Now then, I'm sure you know why I invited you here?"

"I don't remember accepting an invitation to be caged," the Great Auk said quietly.

"Cage? These are our finest guest accommodations!

You're welcome to leave at any time—my friend Feathertop will show you out."

Rozbell hooted again as Feathertop swooped down, grasped Lockley's cage with his massive talons, and shook it violently. Lockley fell backward, stricken with fear.

"Now, old bird," said Rozbell. "I know Sedna is behind the Mystery of the Disappearing Fish. And I know that *you* know how to appease Sedna. You must. It's what old birds like you are for."

The Great Auk said nothing, and Rozbell had one of his house sparrows fetch him a scroll. "We have *ways*, you know," the king continued, unfurling the scroll. "How does being tied to a tree while a pair of woodpeckers drum on your head grab you? Or we could tie you down, cover you with honey, then cover you with honey-eating insects, and *then* sic a honey-eating-insect–eating insectivore on you! One of those long tongues darting in and out all over your body—the tickling would drive you mad!"

"You want to cover me with honey and insects for the sole purpose of tickling me?" said the Great Auk, which enraged Rozbell.

"Do you want your colony to starve?" he screeched.

"I trust the colony to care for itself," said the Great Auk, "but if that tragedy were to come to pass, it would be preferable to living as an owl's slave."

Rozbell became so overheated he started panting. From

his own cage, Lockley could only admire the difference between these two leaders—one courageous and calm, the other a sputtering tyrant. He noticed that even Astra seemed to be looking at the Great Auk with something like fascination.

"Astra!" barked Rozbell, snapping the snowy owl back to attention. "Describe for our honored guest here how the auks are starving, how they are begging for food, wondering why *the Great Auk* isn't there to help them."

Before Astra could respond, Rozbell carried on. "I can picture them now," he said, his tail flicking, "crying their beady eyes out, especially those ridiculous puffins with those weird little triangles for eyes. . . ."

"See here!" said Lockley. "Is that entirely necessary?"

Rozbell stopped cackling and flew back over to Lockley's cage. "I'd almost forgotten about you. What do *you* think about the old bird's refusal to stand up for his colony?" he said, nodding his head at the Great Auk.

Lockley could feel his legs shake as he tried to stare into the owl's penetrating eyes. But he cleared his throat and said as confidently as he could, "I think the Great Auk is standing up for us quite well, thank you."

"*Quite well, thank you!*" mocked Rozbell in a high-pitched voice, and then he dropped to the ground and began repeating the phrase over and over as he waddled in a circle, presumably making fun of the way puffins walked. "Quite well, quite well . . . *gewh, gewh, gewh!*"

Lockley and the Great Auk looked at each other, knowing there was no telling what Rozbell would do next—and nothing they could do about it. Finally the pygmy owl flew back to the Great Auk's cage.

"Let's be reasonable," he said with rigid calm. "You help me appease Sedna, and then you and that one can go back to Neversink and live peacefully. Is the fish tax and a few smidgens really too much to bear?"

"A few smidgens?" said the Great Auk. "A few smidgens, perhaps. But I believe you are the one unable to be content with just a *few* smidgens."

"Fine," said Rozbell through a clenched beak. "A *lot* of smidgens. May I remind everyone that Tytonia faces a potentially devastating food crisis?" he added, spinning his head to the trees behind him before turning back to the Great Auk. "*I'm* trying to feed my flock. You're willing to let not just owls starve, but *your* birds too!"

Lockley had to admit Rozbell had a way with words. Twisting them, that is. But the Great Auk was unmoved. "As I've tried to tell you, I have complete confidence that my colony can take care of themselves. There are birds of great courage and determination there," he said, looking toward Lockley. "Without me, another leader will emerge.

In fact, perhaps it's time that happened."

"How very noble," said Rozbell. "Allow me to oblige you. *Feathertop!*"

As Feathertop spread his wings, the Great Auk said, "I could make you a deal." Rozbell halted the eagle for the moment, and the Great Auk continued, "That is . . . if you are genuinely concerned about your food supply, and not just using this as a chance to throttle Neversink. I would help appease Sedna, and for as long as Tytonia's food supply is thought to be in jeopardy, Neversink, as an independent colony, would agree to supply you with fish—*raw* fish, not smidgens—until it is determined that the Sickness has not returned, or has passed."

Rozbell just stared at him. Astra looked at the king, curious as to how he would wriggle free. The king had never stopped asserting that he believed the Sickness was a real threat.

"To borrow a phrase," said the Great Auk, "do you want *your* birds to starve?"

Rozbell spun his head around the owlery and saw that everyone, from the house sparrows to his servant owl to Astra and Feathertop, was waiting for him to respond.

"This is a trick!" he blurted. "Everyone knows the old ones are tricksters. Feathertop!" The martial eagle swept down next to his master. "I need to hunt and then rest. But I want you to stand here licking your chops in front of the fish-eaters until I return. Take a good look, Great Auk. Because come next dusk-fall, I'm going to have Feathertop carve your little puffin friend up piece by piece, as painfully as possible, while you watch. It will be sort of symbolic of what you're doing to your whole colony by your selfishness. I love symbolism, don't you?"

"You mean like how your tiny stature symbolizes all your shortcomings as a leader?" the Great Auk asked.

Rozbell inflated with rage, looking as if he was going to explode into a shower of tawny feathers. Lockley thought for sure Rozbell would have Feathertop kill them both right away. Instead Rozbell shut his eyes tight for a moment, perhaps to prevent a spasm of blinking, before opening them wide again and saying, "This isn't Neversink—the sun *will* set on you!"

A late morning breeze through the Midland Woods sent the Great Auk's and Lockley's cages swaying gently back and forth, turning them into pendulums counting down the minutes until their own demise.

Neither bird attempted to talk as long as the menacing Feathertop sat there, staring at them with his reptilian eyes. After a time, though, Feathertop looked around, surveying the trees, and then took off.

"Rozbell must be a heavy sleeper," croaked the Great Auk, "or Feathertop wouldn't risk getting caught leaving us unguarded."

Lockley couldn't help notice how weak the Great Auk sounded, and how weary he looked. "With all due respect, you don't look as if you could manage much even if he left our cages open."

"The eagle wasn't gentle with me, to be sure. And I'm not strong anymore. I need the spray of the sea in my nostrils."

"I have to confess something," said Lockley. "I didn't intend to anger Sedna. But when I realized what had happened, I was almost . . . glad. Glad to deprive Rozbell of what he wanted. Maybe even a little glad to make the rest of the colony suffer as much as Lucy had. Apparently I grossly underestimated Rozbell's obsession with smidgens."

"It's not just that," said the Great Auk. "His grudge against the colony runs deep. The same is true of many Owls With Hats. For some, ancestors were lost during the Cod Wars. Others were merely raised to hate auks. It's a sickness in its own right."

"I guess my appreciation of history isn't quite as advanced as you thought," Lockley admitted. "And now I've caused all this misery."

"No," the Great Auk replied firmly. "Rozbell caused all this misery, and he did so deliberately. You must remember that. Your mixed feelings were understandable. But your plan was to help the colony, ultimately. And I must say, it was a courageous thing to try."

"Foolish is more like it," said Lockley. "But despite

Rozbell's unwillingness to take your deal, we have no proof that the Sickness isn't a real threat. Maybe Rozbell's intentions—at least originally—were good."

"I admire your empathy, Lockley. A wonderful quality in any creature, but especially a leader."

Lockley snorted, but the Great Auk ignored him. "It really doesn't matter where the fish went, or why. Sedna can bring them back. She must be appealed to."

"Ah yes," said Lockley timidly. "I was actually on my way to your nest to discuss it with you when we were captured. I confess, I needed your help remembering the story."

"'The Tricking of Sedna.'"

"*Tricking!*" Lockley exclaimed. "That's it!"

The Great Auk said nothing, until Lockley pressed him. "If we do have only one afternoon to live, I'd love to hear another story."

Despite his weakened state and the small dimensions of his cage, the Great Auk raised himself up before he began to speak.

"We all know to give thanks to Sedna for keeping our waters rich with fish. The youngest auks learn to memorize the thanksgivings from their parents. But what many forget is that Sedna is anything but a benevolent goddess. The birds should fear her. In a way, it was only because of the seabirds that Sedna became a goddess. But it all came about because of trickery, and thus the birds never fully had her trust. She is easily angered by us and quick to punish.

"It all goes back to the petrel, the sky roamer and sea glider that nests at the very top of the sea cliffs. None have been welcome on Neversink for a very long time, in part to appease Sedna. For Sedna, you see, was made by the gods. They sent her to live on an island in the north, but without companionship, and she was lonely. She wasn't immortal, like her creators, nor was she like the other animals. She had bare skin and long, slender limbs. She walked on her two legs, and was earthbound. The birds simply described her as 'one made in the gods' own image.' She was a divine experiment. And one day a petrel spied her, sitting on the shore of her isolated home, staring out to sea.

"Petrels are proud birds, but this one was especially proud. He was a *storm* petrel, and could summon great winds and roil the waters with his wings. Sedna's smooth brown skin and flowing dark hair captivated him, and he decided then and there he had found a mate worthy of him. But because she was not a bird, he came to her in disguise. He made a mask of carved ivory to hide his beak and a cloak of sealskin to cover his feathers, and he approached her from the sea in a canoe made of bark. When she saw him, he sang to her:

Come to me,
Come into the land of the birds,

Where there is never hunger,
Where my tent is made of beautiful skins.
You will have a necklace of ivory
And sleep on the skins of bears.
Your lamps will always be filled with oil,
And your pot with meat.

"She was drawn to him, and so enchanted she couldn't see that there was no tent, nor were there skins of bears, but only an open nest at the top of the sea cliffs. Until one morning, when, thinking she was asleep, the petrel removed his disguise to fly out to sea. But Sedna saw him, and the scales fell from her eyes. She saw her new home for what it was and felt the lash of the wind.

"While the petrel was gone, Sedna tried to escape. She climbed down from the sea cliffs and found the small boat. She rowed out to sea, toward Ocean's End, thinking the petrel would not pursue her into the coldest lands. But when he returned and discovered what had happened, he was consumed by anger. His spy birds told him where she was, and he followed her toward Ocean's End.

"Once he saw her, he began beating his wings, summoning great crests of waves that swamped the little boat. Sedna sank into the freezing waters, but tried to save herself. Each time, however, that she reached the surface and grabbed the edge of the boat, the tips of her frozen fingers would snap off like icicles, until finally she had nothing left with which to grab. She sank to the bottom, her raven hair fanning out like squid ink, her severed fingers and thumbs swimming off with the currents.

"The gods took pity on their creation. Her broken digits became the seals, whales, and walruses. Sedna was given dominion over them and the fish of the northern seas, but she cursed her fate and became a vindictive sea goddess. If angered, she withholds the bounty of the sea. The seabirds have ever been mindful of this."

Speaking for so long had drained the Great Auk, and he rested for several minutes. He was about to continue when Feathertop came crashing through the branches and landed in the glade with a small deer in his talons. Lockley watched with horror as the eagle ripped huge strips of flesh from the deer with his terrible beak. The Great Auk noticed, too.

"I wouldn't want your suffering on my conscience," he said.

Lockley swallowed hard before answering. "No. You shouldn't give in to Rozbell."

Feathertop quickly put an end to their conversation by flying at Lockley's cage and savagely biting one of the bars, staining it with deer blood. Lockley crouched in terror and said nothing more until the sun began to set and Rozbell returned.

"Ah, dusk-fall," sang Rozbell, perched like a pinecone

on the tip of a branch. "My favorite time of day. The owls come awake, and the miserable groundlings start running for their lives. How can you stand to live in a place with no shadows? No grayness? Everything on Neversink is so . . . black-and-white." Rozbell pretended to shiver with disgust. "Of course, one does tire of the same old thing. I, for one, am tired of eating food with fur on it: moles, voles, bats, rats, mice, shrews . . . to say nothing of songbirds, lizards, and bugs!"

Lockley had to admit, that did sound distasteful. Still, he certainly wasn't tired of eating fish. Rozbell hopped onto a branch closer to the Great Auk. "That's why I'm going to give you another day to think about giving me what I want. Surely we can learn to compromise?"

"Can you?" said the Great Auk. Feathertop flew toward his cage and swatted it with his massive wing. The cage spun wildly, and the Great Auk collapsed to the floor.

"That wasn't a very nice thing to say to someone who just spared your life," said Rozbell. "For now." And off he went, leaving Lockley and the Great Auk to wonder what the devious pygmy owl was up to.

MISSING

"How could Lockley not tell us where he was going?" said Egbert.

"We didn't tell anyone where *we* were going," Ruby reminded him.

"That's entirely different," said Egbert. "It would be hard to lose track of the only walrus in a colony of birds."

"That's true," Ruby agreed. "Believe me, they've tried."

Egbert was down on his forefins, rocking through the sand along the shore while Ruby glided next to him. They were searching the beach and rocks where Lockley had last crashed into them. He had been gone almost two days and Lucy had told them she was worried.

"The fool bird has probably broken his neck trying to soar again," said Egbert, his gruff tone unable to hide his concern.

"I don't see him anywhere," said Ruby, who was zigzagging off in all directions for quick looks.

Suddenly Egbert pulled up and sat back on his ample tail section.

"What's the matter?" said Ruby. "Do you smell food?"

"No. It's just . . . come with me. . . ." And Egbert led them to the other end of the colony and to the Great Auk's nest, where he knew Lockley sometimes went when he needed counsel. Something Egbert found strange, since he was forever offering counsel on any number of matters on a regular basis.

When they arrived, they found the nest in disarray, littered with black-and-white feathers, loose tea leaves, and broken dishes. More alarming still, they found white feathers that were unmistakably those of a snowy owl, as well as large brown feathers they assumed to be those of an eagle. "Oh dear," said Egbert.

It took Lucy a long time to come to the door when Egbert and Ruby reported back to her. Both were stunned by how much weaker she looked, and Egbert hoped she would soon lay her egg for fear that if she got any frailer, the strain would do her in.

"We need to show you something," and he handed her

the black-and-white feathers that he had collected from the Great Auk's nest. Birds have an uncanny ability to recognize their mate's plumage. Lucy took the handful of feathers and began sorting them. Most belonged to the Great Auk, but there were two she pulled aside and held close to her bill. "These are Lockley's," she said.

Egbert sighed deeply, but then put on a brave face. "Don't you worry, my dear. At least we know what happened to them. Which means we can figure out what needs to be done. And they must be okay. Rozbell wouldn't have dragged them across the ocean just to, you know . . ."

"Off them," said Ruby.

"Why don't you learn some tact?" said Egbert.

"Why don't you learn to get to the point?" said Ruby.

Their brief bickering actually made Lucy smile. It was, well, *normal.* But then they heard a commotion from somewhere else in the colony. Not normal auk commotion—something was definitely wrong. Once they made their way to the scene of the disturbance, what they saw took them by surprise. It was Astra, surrounded by a crew of burrowing owls. The snowy owl appeared to be arguing with the crew leader, a cross burrowing owl with his black hat cocked to one side.

The first thing Egbert, Ruby, and Lucy heard was the owl with the cocked hat telling Astra, "Rozbell didn't send me to be your messenger. I'm in charge of my crew." Astra ground her beak but maintained her composure. The crew leader, named Edmund, turned to the gathering crowd of auks. "One of those old owls who knows everything told Rozbell that Arctic creatures often store up food for the winter. Would be just like an auk to squirrel away food like . . . well, like a *squirrel*." Edmund motioned to the burrowing owls—tiny, long-legged owls with a knack for digging. "Search every burrow, nest, nook, and cranny for fish," he commanded. "Fresh fish, dried fish, pickled fish, or fish parts. We know these greedy *fish-eaters* are keeping fish from His Majesty!"

The burrowing owls dispersed and invaded, their chucking and chattering mixing with the hissing and growling of angry auks into one shrill chorus. Flitting from nest to nest up and down the sea cliffs, they used their stiltlike legs to dig through the auks' possessions with reckless abandon. This was bad enough for the guillemots and puffins; you can imagine how angry it made the higher-living auks, the razorbills and murres, to see their personal possessions tossed onto the rocks below.

"We don't store fish!" protested one. "We catch what we eat every day!" Which was true, especially now that the fish were dwindling. The meager amounts that any auk had been able to catch in the past two days had been consumed immediately.

The fact that the burrowing owls were not finding any

fish began to frustrate Edmund. Prancing among the mess, looking at various auk items, Edmund held up a sealskin with crude drawings of auks and owls on it. "What's this?" he wondered aloud.

"It's a tapestry, depicting the Cod Wars," said a razorbill. "It's mine."

Edmund looked at it with scorn. "Hmm. Revisionist history, I'm sure," but instead of giving it back to the razorbill, he tossed it onto a pile with other items he had picked out, like a warm goose-down blanket yanked from a nest and a set of small, milky-white figurines carved from walrus tusk. "Much too nice for an auk," he muttered several times, putting things he liked to one side.

And then, above the din came the wail of a guillemot. A mournful, solitary wail, unmistakably that of a mother. She was among those who had already laid their eggs, and one of the burrowing owls had carelessly kicked her egg out of its nest and sent it rolling through the door. Fortunately, guillemots, like puffins, are ground dwellers, so instead of plunging down the cliff face, the egg rolled along a grassy patch and against a rock, unharmed. But the mother's distress had arrested everyone's attention, including Egbert's. He turned to Lucy and said, "Get back in your burrow, my dear."

"What's the matter, Egbert?" But instead of explaining, Egbert gently urged her inside with one of his fins.

"What's up, E?" said Ruby.

"Just scram," he said, and as the owls came closer, Egbert sprawled in front of Lucy's door along the rocks, blocking all evidence of a burrow. "Just taking the air," he said lightly as the small owls scampered by. Some even used him as a landing pad as they hopped out of nests from the cliff face above. Once they had gone by, Ruby returned.

"Nice use of your flab," she said.

"I have a bad feeling about this," he said. "One or two snowy owls hanging around is one thing. Now a small army of burrowing owls? Did you see how reckless they were with that poor guillemot's egg? I think the less Rozbell knows about Lucy, including where she lives, whether she's breeding, or even that she's Lockley's mate, the better. Of course, there's no telling what that snowy owl has told him." He looked at Astra, who seemed almost as annoyed as the auks to have burrowing owls underfoot.

Once the owls had finished their search, Edmund collected some things he thought Rozbell would like into a nice pile, then turned to Astra. "Guard this," he said. "I'll send a pelican back for it." Edmund flew off with his crew, leaving behind a colony still buzzing with agitation and fear. If they had been slow to appreciate Lockley's warnings about the danger Rozbell posed to their way of life, they were beginning to now.

"Ruby, we've got to do something," said Egbert, after

the two had retreated to Egbert's shelter. "Lucy needs protection, and the colony needs a leader."

"I'm one step ahead of you," said Ruby. "A rescue mission to spring Lockley and the Great Auk!"

"Or how about this," said Egbert. "*I* could assume leadership of the colony, and you could protect Lucy."

Ruby tweaked him on the snout.

"Ow!"

"I thought you wanted to *help* the colony," she said.

"Fine, then. How do you propose we rescue them?"

"We?" said Ruby. "For one thing, I don't propose that we have a blubbery walrus go slogging through the woods of Tytonia. We may as well send a note ahead of time announcing our arrival."

Egbert's face was as red as a bee sting. "I assume you have a plan?"

Ruby shrugged. "I'll think of something on the way."

"*Think of something on the way?* You call that a plan?"

"What would you call it?"

"I'd call it folly," said Egbert. "It wonderfully captures your naive heroism coupled with the complete hopelessness of the situation."

"Thanks for the vote of confidence."

From above came the disapproving click of a beak. They looked up to see Astra perched on a high rock, eavesdropping. "Whatever you're thinking of doing, I wouldn't," she said coolly. "Unless you want to end up caged in the Green-Golden Wood alongside your friend and leader."

Before either Egbert or Ruby could reply, Astra flew off.

"The Green-Golden Wood?" said Ruby.

"That's where the Great Gray Owl lived," said Egbert. "I would have thought they were taken to Rozbell's owlery, in Slog's Hollow. Unless . . . she's giving us a *clue*."

"I don't have a clue what you're talking about," said Ruby.

"Then again," mused Egbert, "a creature as intelligent as a snowy owl would be intelligent enough to know that I am more intelligent still, and so she might be telling us something she *thinks* we want to hear. Or thinks we *think* we want to hear."

Egbert rubbed his chin thoughtfully and then looked to Ruby for affirmation, but she had already gone.

The afternoon following their stay of execution, Lockley and the Great Auk sat watching Feathertop exercise his beak by snapping bones in two. The sickening crunch was too much to bear, so Lockley shut his eyes and tried to focus on happier times, like those lazy afternoons he once enjoyed with Lucy, taking their tea and enjoying cranberry scones or fish smidgens. *Smidgens.* He never wanted to so much as smell another one again. That's what had started this mess; the once pleasant memory was ruined.

Snap. Crunch.

It was no use. Lockley was left to wonder if Rozbell might at least agree to return his remains to Neversink, so that Lucy could bury him at sea.

The sea, the sea!

That's what he wanted. The sea was where he belonged. Those funny shapes and awkward moving parts that made puffins so comical on land revealed their harmonious purpose underwater. Below the surface, their short, powerful wings and broad webbed feet propelled their torpedo-shaped bodies deep into the ocean's twilight zone, and their oversized bills allowed them to capture dozens of fish per dive. Survival challenges that would cripple an eagle were elegantly and skillfully met by the humble puffin. *If only we never had to return to land,* Lockley often thought, *our self-esteem would be much higher.* There would have been no need for foolish dreams of soaring.

Lockley opened his eyes in time to see Feathertop flying out of the grove. "What happened?"

"I'm not sure," said the Great Auk. "Something startled him, but I didn't see what."

"I bet I know what it was," said Ruby, suddenly appearing in midair next to Lockley's head.

"Not now, Ruby," said Lockley instinctively, and then: "Ruby! For the love of fish!" Lockley never thought he'd be so happy to see his pesky friend, and he would have hugged her, except that it's physically impossible for a puffin and a hummingbird to embrace.

"We don't have much time until Featherbrain is back from his wild hummingbird chase," said Ruby. And with surprising agility, she began unlashing the vine that locked the door to Lockley's cage with her bill.

"Hurry—the Great Auk," said Lockley when he was free, but before Ruby could begin, the Great Auk said, "No."

"No?"

"It will be hard enough for a bird as conspicuous as a puffin to escape from these woods," said the Great Auk. "The addition of an elderly, injured bird my size would be fatal."

Lockley didn't know what to say, but the Great Auk added, "Lockley, the end of the story . . . 'The Tricking of Sedna.' The only way to appease her is with the spirit journey."

"The spirit journey," repeated Lockley.

"Yes, and it's not for the faint of heart," said the Great Auk. "Of course, her wrath is directed at Neversink. You could take Lucy elsewhere. Start over."

From beyond the trees came the loud *kloo-ee, kloo-ee, kloo-ee* of an enraged Feathertop.

"Let's go," said Ruby, and after exchanging a brief look with the Great Auk, Lockley followed Ruby out of the grove.

DOWN THE BADGER HOLE

Lockley ran as fast as he could, afraid he wouldn't be able to fly through the dense stand of trees. His wide, webbed feet managed to trample every twig, stick, and fallen branch, making it sound like a hundred seabirds were stampeding through the forest. Finally he collapsed by a tree, exhausted. "Ruby, it's no use," he panted. "Even if I didn't stick out so much, birds of prey have exceptional hearing."

From high above a voice said, "A deaf bird could have heard you just now."

Lockley and Ruby looked up, but neither of them saw anything. That is, until Otus, the scops owl, stepped out onto the branch he was perched on. He had been perfectly camouflaged next to the tree trunk.

"An owl!" blurted Ruby. "Run, Lockley, run!"

Lockley struggled to his feet and tried to run again, but promptly tripped over a stick and fell on his face.

"There's not much point in running now that I've seen you," said Otus as he dropped to the ground. "Besides, I'm here to help you, not capture you."

"Why would an owl want to help us?" said Lockley.

"I know that whatever you did has at least temporarily stopped Rozbell from harvesting food from Neversink," said Otus. "And seeing Rozbell fail is in the interest of some."

"But if the Sickness is real, aren't you worried about starving?"

"Some of us think Rozbell in power is worse."

"Hey, same here!" said Ruby.

Lockley shook his head. "Both owls and auks may come to regret that position."

Otus hooted. "I can lead you back to your cage if you wish. Or I can help you escape."

"Escape!" said Ruby. "Pick escape!" She hovered next to Otus. "That camouflage thing you did up in the tree. I've seen insects do that in the jungle. What can we disguise Lockley as, Mr. Owl?"

Otus hooted again. "Unless a parcel of penguins happens by, you're out of luck."

"Indeed," said Lockley, trying to hide his irritation.

"No, I have a different sort of concealment in mind," said Otus, and clicked his beak twice. A small mound of dirt appeared at their feet.

"What's this?" said Lockley, leaning in for a closer look. Out popped a tiny, furry face with pinhole eyes. "Ah! What the devil?"

"I should wonder the same thing," said the mole. "What's a penguin doing on Tytonia?"

"I am not a penguin! There *are* no penguins on Tytonia! I am a puffin!"

"There aren't any puffins on Tytonia either," said the mole. "And yet, here you are."

"Touché," said Ruby.

"Good sir," said the mole. "You mustn't take offense. My eyesight's quite poor, you know."

"Don't worry, he gets that all the time," said Ruby.

"There's only one sure way for you to leave the Midland Woods without detection," said Otus.

"And what would that be?" Lockley wondered. At which point the mole pointed at the hole he had just come from. "You can't possibly expect me to squeeze myself into a mole hole?"

"Oh dear me," said the mole, shaking his head. "I'm afraid you've taken me too literally."

"Well, most animals are fairly literal," said Lockley. "Apparently, it's why we don't yet have a large body of imaginative fiction."

Ruby just stared at him. "You've definitely been spending too much time with Egbert."

"As I was saying," the mole continued, "I meant you should go underground in general. Below the Midland Woods are miles and miles of badger tunnels."

"I can already spot a flaw in that plan," said Ruby.

"What's that?" said the mole.

"Um—running into badgers?"

The mole chuckled. "Oh no, these are ancient tunnels, abandoned after the old Weasel Wars. Crude compared to modern badger burrows, but big enough for a squidgy seabird like yourself."

"I know it sounds dangerous," said Otus, "but so are Rozbell and Feathertop."

"I don't mean to seem ungrateful," said Lockley, "but do you mind if Ruby and I discuss this?"

Otus bowed slightly. "I wouldn't waste too much time deciding, though."

Lockley took Ruby aside, but she was impatient with his hesitation. "Lockley, I don't like it any more than you, but if you could have seen Neversink when I left. Owls everywhere! And not just any owls. Owls wearing hats! Owls wearing hats who hate auks!"

"Technically that's redundant," said Lockley. Ruby tweaked him between the eyes. "Ow!"

"Do you know how easy you'll be to spot aboveground?"

"In other words," said Lockley, "what choice do we have?"

"Finally," said Ruby, buzzing back to Otus and the mole.

And so they thanked Otus for his help and followed the mole through the woods until they came to what looked like an ordinary blanket of dirt and leaves near some shrubs in the undergrowth. Looking closer, though, Lockley found it to be the covering of a hole—a hole large enough for a puffin and, he presumed, a badger.

"Who's first?" said the mole.

"You're still leading the way, aren't you?" said Lockley. "After you." And down the badger hole they went.

What little light filtered from above quickly disappeared once they entered the tunnel. This was familiar territory for the mole, who was used to crawling underground, navigating with his nose. For Lockley and Ruby, it was downright spooky. Lockley, who lived in a burrow and hunted fish in the ocean's twilight zone, had expected to have more use of his senses, but this was something else.

"I think I just discovered that I'm afraid of the dark," said Ruby.

"Oh, dear me," said the mole. "I forget you two aren't diggers." And he scampered back up out of the hole and was gone for several minutes, forcing Lockley to conclude that moles left something to be desired as guides. But eventually he did return, carrying with him a large wad of what appeared to be glow-in-the-dark moss.

"It's fox fire," he explained. "It's a bioluminescent fungus."

"Ewww, fungus," said Ruby.

"Brilliant!" said Lockley, and turning back down the tunnel, he admired the dim light created by the fox fire. "There are sea creatures like this in the twilight zone. Come on then."

The mole led them through a maze of winding passageways, and occasionally Lockley noticed recesses in the earthen walls, often stacked with bones. He held the fox fire torch up to one of the crypts, the amber glow illuminating a fierce skull baring its teeth.

"Ancient remains," said the mole, when Lockley jumped back. "Most from the Weasel Wars. The badgers didn't have the luxury of burying their dead on the battlefields, as was their custom at the time. So they buried them in the walls of their secret tunnels. As the battles got bloodier, these tunnels became extensive underground tombs."

Lockley heard Ruby hovering closer to his head.

"Don't worry, Ruby. I don't believe in ghosts."

"Really?" said the mole. "Badgers sure do. They believe that if the bones are missing from any of these chambers, the spirit of the warrior has been disturbed and roams again."

"Probably just carried off by some other creature. Or decomposed," said Lockley. Still, he felt a prickling sensation as he wandered through the badger catacombs. First the thick woods, now this. He was used to wide-open landscapes with a view for miles, and the fluid boundaries of the sea. Here he felt the tunnel walls closing on him, constricting him, as if he had been swallowed by a giant serpent.

"Are you okay, Lockley?" Ruby wondered, noticing that Lockley seemed to be wobbling worse than usual.

"Fine."

"Want to see something interesting?" said the mole. "A little off the track I was taking you, but what's the difference, as long as you're not up there with the owls?"

Lockley didn't like the sound of it, but his breath was coming in gulps and he couldn't object before the mole steered them left, descending even lower into the earth. The lower they went, the narrower the tunnel felt to Lockley, who feared he would pass out. To his great relief, however, the tunnel soon opened up into an enormous underground cavern, and the cold, clammy air suddenly seemed fresher and more breathable.

The cave was lit, but Lockley couldn't tell how—either from a hole in the ground far above or with other bioluminescent organisms like the fox fire. He didn't care—he had room to stretch his wings and fresh air to fill his lungs.

He looked around the cave, where stalactites from the ceiling and stalagmites from the floor came together like teeth. And in the center was an enormous limestone statue of a badger, seated on a throne of roots and holding a gnarled scepter.

"Is this a tomb also?" said Ruby.

"A temple," said the mole. "The statue is of the great badger king Theodorus. The one who led them to victory in the War of the Trees. They couldn't actually bury him here, of course. The body would have been stolen. No one knows what happened to his bones. Pretty amazing, I'm sure you'll agree."

Indeed, Lockley had never seen anything like it. He couldn't imagine the Great Auk wanting them to carve an idol of him, let alone one ten times his actual size. Even the owls had never created such a thing. Lockley couldn't decide whether to be awed or disgusted.

"Well, I guess that's enough sightseeing," said the mole, which was an odd thing for a nearly blind animal to say. "I imagine you two are ready to get out of here."

Lockley started backing away from the statue, unable to completely look away, when he felt a pair of long claws grasp his shoulders from behind. "Ruby, did you suddenly grow large talons?"

"I'm over here!"

Lockley slowly turned around and found himself

looking up into the small eyes of a large animal. The badger was squatting on his powerful hind legs, his massive back spread like the hood of a cobra. His trademark white stripes were there, but the surrounding fur had turned nearly as white. He twitched his short, whiskered snout at Lockley.

"What's going on?" called the mole. "I smell fear."

"B-badger ghost," Lockley said, almost whispering. And then, much louder, "Badger ghost! Badger ghost!" He tried to run for one of the tunnels but forgot to duck and hit his head, falling backward. The badger jumped on top of him, baring a set of well-worn teeth in Lockley's face.

"I'm no ghost," he growled, "but I'll make one of you if you don't tell me what you're doing here! Did the weasels send you?"

"What? Weasels? No!" Lockley sputtered.

"We're dodging owls," said Ruby.

"Owls!" spat the badger. "Weasels with wings!" He jumped off Lockley and scratched his ear with his hind leg. Lockley could see how worn his claws were. Even his teeth had lost some of their bite. In fact, he was not a ghost, but a very old badger, and possibly a senile one.

"Are you here to see King Theodorus?" said the badger. "Never was there a fiercer fighter of weasels—winged or not!" He scratched his other ear with his other foot.

Ruby buzzed toward the statue. "You do realize this is just a piece of rock?" To prove her point, she pecked at the

limestone head with her bill, sending a tiny echo ringing off the cave walls.

"That's just to fool them!" the badger explained, running toward Ruby. "I wore my claws to the nub helping carve that." He admired the statue while Ruby and Lockley looked to the mole for guidance.

"Good sir," said the mole gently, "the Weasel Wars have been over for decades. Theodorus is long dead—"

"Wars never end!" snarled the badger. "It would be just like a weasel to lie in wait for years, lulling us into a false sense of security."

"Us?" the mole wondered. He didn't smell anyone else around.

"Yes," the badger replied. "A small band of us still loyal to Theodorus. Unlike the *others*, who *fled*."

"Mr. Badger," said Lockley, "we didn't mean to intrude. May we just be on our way?"

The badger scampered back to Lockley and sniffed him. "Hmm. I don't smell weasel." He pulled at Lockley's feathers and wiggled his bill, as if to make sure he wasn't a weasel in disguise. "What's a penguin doing on Tytonia?"

"I am *not*—" Lockley began to erupt, but looking into the elderly badger's crazed eyes, he composed himself. "I am actually a puffin."

"Oh," said the badger. "What's a puffin doing on Tytonia?"

"Well, that's a rather long story," Lockley began, but the badger interrupted.

"Dodging owls, you said, right?"

"We're headed north, actually," said the mole. "Away from the Midland Woods. I'm helping Mr. Puffin and his friend get home."

"North," the badger repeated. And then he pointed to a tunnel behind them. "Take that one then. When you come to the split, follow the sound of the river. Else you'll end up on the moors."

"Thank you," said Lockley, and he grabbed the mole and nodded to Ruby, not wanting to linger. They hurried along the tunnel until they were sure the badger wasn't following them. "What was that all about?"

"Terribly sad, terribly sad," said the mole. "Theodorus was a charismatic leader, so I've heard. I mean, they don't make great big statues to honor shrinking violets, do they? Yes, anyway, after he won the War of the Trees, it was a golden age for the badgers. Theodorus had united all the clans, and they lived low and mighty for many years. Might have gone on forever, except of course, no one lives forever. Theodorus was followed by a series of weak kings, interested really in nothing except the trappings of royalty. No appreciation for how it had all come to be. Took their power for granted. Eventually the clans fragmented again . . . were no match for new enemies when the weasels joined forces with wolverines, skunks, ferrets, otters, and minks. Entire clans died out."

"How do you know all this?" said Lockley.

"My ancestors," said the mole. "Moles are fellow tunnel dwellers, of course. We were often used for spying during the wars. My father always thought it instructive for us lowly earth eaters to study how the mighty can fall."

"So the badger kingdom split up and the different clans had to move elsewhere," said Lockley. "But what about that poor thing back there?"

"Never seen anything like it," said the mole. "I don't use these old tunnels very often. But I guess there were survivors and diehards who remained. In a way, he is a kind of ghost, really. Don't you think?"

They continued to meander through the tunnels, the history lesson distracting Lockley from his claustrophobia. "What was that about owls being weasels?" he asked.

"Oh, that," said the mole. "Owls . . . birds in general, really . . . a bit of a superior attitude, you know—no offense to you, good sir! But the Parliament of Owls is forever trying to extend its dominion. They are the rulers of all birds on Tytonia, but the larger beasts of the ground have never recognized their authority."

"How nice for them," said Lockley, somewhat bitterly.

"Yes, anyway," the mole continued, "every now and again they try to form alliances, to curry favor with the toothy beasts. So it was during the Weasel Wars, when the Great Gray Owl tried to help the weasels against Theodorus."

"Why?" said Lockley. "What was in it for the owls?"

"You didn't hear it from me," said the mole, nervously tapping his forepaws together, "but weasels and their kin are devious. Clever, in a dangerous sort of way. And they can go anywhere—underground, underwater, into trees. I suppose the owls thought they would be useful allies."

"Devious and everywhere—owls *are* weasels with wings!" said Ruby. "What's that?" She zoomed ahead into the darkness, then called back, "I think I hear water!" Lockley and the mole heard it too, finally, as they came to a place where the tunnel split off in two directions, just as the aged badger had said.

"It sounds like the river is this way," said Lockley, stepping toward the leftmost tunnel.

"No, no," said the mole, going right. "This way. Trust me, I know these passageways better than some deranged relic of badger-glory past."

"But—"

"Come on, then," said the mole, disappearing into the tunnel.

Lockley wondered if the mole was really any less crazy than the badger. Living underground, surrounded by walls, had to do something to your brain, didn't it? But he had no choice unless he and Ruby wanted to strike out on their own, so he scurried after the mole, carrying his fox fire, which was beginning to lose its luster.

Ruby noticed that the mole pulled up occasionally to dig in the dirt for worms, grubs, and other small insects. "Must maintain my strength!" he said. The hummingbird felt her own tiny stomach rumble and her energy flag, so she asked if she could share. "Of course, of course!" said the mole. "Plenty for everyone!" He dug furiously in the ground and in the sides of the tunnel, producing more than enough wriggling insects for Ruby to inhale. "Mr. Puffin?" he asked, but Lockley shook his head in disgust.

"Must you dig so hard?" Lockley asked. He had started to feel the earthen walls closing in on him again, and watching loose dirt crumble to the floor didn't help his sense of security. But watching the mole eat brought something to his mind. "Mr. Mole, pardon my bluntness, but you are typical prey for many other animals. Have predators been avoiding you? Do you believe the Sickness has returned?"

The mole tapped his forepaws together again. "Well, the Great Gray Owl, rest his soul"—and here, the mole choked up a little—"he wasn't convinced. Lived through it before, you know. The real thing. Doesn't matter now, no sir. The king is dead, and real or not, fear feeds on fear."

"Are you okay, Mr. Mole?"

"Oh yes. Forgive a poor old earth eater." He sniffled twice and collected himself. "I may as well tell you, I did a little spying for the former king. I met him through Otus, actually, which is why he trusts me."

"So owls formed alliances with moles, too?"

"Alliances? Ha-ha, no," said the mole. "More like, trading services in exchange for not being eaten." He laughed nervously again.

Ruby, meanwhile, had ingested so many insects she had to sit down. "If I had on pants, I'd unbutton them," she said.

"There's no such thing as pants," Lockley reminded her.

"Over here," called the mole, who had scampered ahead. "You might not fall behind if you didn't want to discuss every little thing. Never met such chatty creatures."

"Oh, well," said Ruby, "you haven't met our friend Egbert. He's as big as an elephant but twice as annoying. Talks constantly, has an opinion about everything, *super* critical."

"Sounds fascinating," said the mole. "Come on, come on. Badger tunnels are no place for a penguin!"

"Puffin!" said Lockley. "Puffin, puffin!"

"Oh yes—huffin', puffin'—I can take a hint. You're eager to get on with it. Not much farther." And he bounded ahead into the darkness.

THE KING'S FINAL SOLUTION

Astra didn't understand why she had been summoned to Tytonia. Even for her it was a long flight, and that was if she was unburdened. Astra was carrying the bundle of spoils collected by Edmund—the bundle a pelican was supposed to fetch. So now she was an errand bird?

She arrived at Rozbell's owlery near dusk-fall, just as the king was awakening. "Astra, good, you're here," he said sleepily. Feathertop was there, of course, along with Alf and the flock of house sparrows. And Edmund, perched on the ground with his hat cocked to the side.

Astra placed the bundle on the ground and unwrapped it, showing Rozbell the finest sealskin tapestries and ivory carvings Auk's Landing had to offer.

"What is that?" he said.

"The spoils," said Astra. "From Neversink?"

"What? Oh, right. I told Edmund to send a pelican back for that."

Edmund looked at Astra and smiled. Astra turned back to Rozbell. "May I ask, Your Majesty, why you summoned me?"

Rozbell looked at her as if to remind her he didn't need a reason for anything he did. But finally he said, "Because as one of my chief associates, I thought you should be here for this."

The king motioned to Alf, who flew up to Rozbell's perch and gently lifted the black hat from Rozbell's head. The servant owl then fetched a small bundle and pulled forth a bright new object that glowed in the fading dusk light. Rozbell bowed his head slightly, allowing Alf to fit the new hat to his head. He then stood up straight for everyone to see.

Rozbell had commissioned a derby of solid gold, a hat to signify his position as *the* owl among Owls With Hats. He had failed to calculate how much heavier a metal hat would be and promptly collapsed from his perch the first time it was put on his head. Not to be denied, Rozbell had then modified the design with the help of a sharp-clawed ground sloth. He had carved away the brim and the top of the derby, leaving a gold band and two tall spires of gold on either side of the head, encrusted with jewels, like a pair of magnificent ear tufts. He had fashioned a crown.

Rozbell handed Astra a scroll. "Read this."

She opened it and read it.

"I mean aloud, you imbecile!"

Astra looked again at Rozbell in his gold crown, then read aloud: "I, Rozbell, King of the Territory of Tytonia, which includes the colony of Neversink, by the authority vested in Me, by Me, and for Me, hereby declare that my new official title shall be Lord of All the Beasts on Earth and Fishes of the Sea. Which title grants me all the powers previously vested in the King, plus lots of other powers, to be enumerated by Me as I go along."

Rozbell seemed pleased with how his new title sounded. Edmund beamed with approval. Feathertop looked bored.

"Should we perform this ceremony before the Parliament?" said Astra.

"Why bother?" said Rozbell, adjusting his crown. "You're the rule-keeper. That's close enough."

Indeed, thought Astra. Governor of an island she had no authority over. And rule-keeper of a parliament that no longer had any rules.

"There's more," said Rozbell. "Everyone, follow me to the prisoners."

Rozbell, Feathertop, Edmund, and Astra flew to the

Green-Golden Wood, and Astra was the first one to see Lockley's cage hanging empty. Feathertop was next, and the massive eagle pulled up short, both angry and alarmed. Rozbell surveyed the scene and then perched on a branch near the Great Auk.

"What's going on?" said Edmund.

Rozbell turned to Feathertop. "When did this happen? I summoned you to my owlery not even an hour ago! Did this happen while you were on guard, and you just didn't tell me? Do you expect me to believe he escaped in the time I allowed you to witness my crowning?"

Feathertop was speechless, shaking his head.

Astra tried to diffuse the situation. "You said it yourself, Your Majesty. The old birds are tricksters. He must have created a diversion."

"In any case," Edmund cut in, "we have spies everywhere, and owls from Falcon Crest to the highlands."

"He will be caught, Your Majesty," said Astra. "He sticks out like a goldfinch, and he can't outfly a bird of prey in the open. Besides, we still have the Great Auk, the one who can tell us about Sedna."

To everyone's surprise, Rozbell had regained his composure, and appeared calm. He leaned forward on his perch and looked the Great Auk straight in the eyes. "Yes, but torturing his friend—his apprentice?—in front of him was our best way to get him to talk. Being forced to watch suffering with your own eyes is far more effective than some abstract notion of your faraway colony starving, isn't it, old bird?"

The Great Auk tried to stare back, but his eyes drifted to the king's gaudy crown. Rozbell threw his head back and hooted. "Not to worry. I think I've come up with something even better." He flitted to a different branch and gestured to Edmund. "My trusty burrowing owl friend here gave me a marvelous idea."

When Edmund beamed, Rozbell added, "Accidentally." Edmund's smirk disappeared, but Rozbell turned to Astra and said, "Of course, even helping accidentally is better than not helping at all."

Astra said nothing. Rozbell addressed the Great Auk again.

"You see, I gave you and your friend an extra day to live because I was convinced the auks were hoarding fish and hiding it from me. Hoarding and hiding. I wouldn't need you to appease Sedna if I could come up with more fish on my own, would I?"

The Great Auk remained stoic, but Rozbell's chirpiness was making him fearful.

"I sent the burrowing owls to root through your nests, and unfortunately, it turns out you auks were telling the truth. Imagine that!" said Rozbell, hooting again. "Poor Edmund was so frustrated . . . he so wants to please me." (Edmund wasn't sure whether to smile at this or not.) "So frustrated, he blurted out, 'Your Majesty, the auks keep nothing in their nests except eggs!'"

The Great Auk slowly shook his head.

"What? No witty remarks this time?" sneered Rozbell.

"Don't you understand?" said the Great Auk. "Even if I told you how to appease Sedna, you wouldn't be able to. She is *our* goddess, not yours."

Rozbell laughed. "Oh, I don't care about appeasing Sedna anymore."

"So you've given up any pretense that this is about protecting your territory from some phantom plague?" The Great Auk's voice was hard as stone now. "You are sadistic."

"On the contrary," said Rozbell. "Well, I *may* be sadistic, but this is most definitely about food. We all know how nutritious eggs are." Rozbell started cackling. "Eating your eggs! What a delicious idea! What an *eggcellent* idea!"

He continued to laugh maniacally. The Great Auk stepped back in his cage, as if stunned that he had underestimated Rozbell's hatred of auks. Watching from her perch, Astra felt her gizzard go sour. She knew what the Great Auk was thinking—auks produced but one egg per couple each breeding season. This wasn't about food, it was about destroying an entire generation of auks.

"You did say it might be better to perish than to live as an owl's slave, didn't you?" said Rozbell. "Well, think of me as the Magic Owl, granting your wish." He pretended to pull a hat off his head and draw wishes from it, all the while chirping, "*Gewh, gewh, gewh! Gewh, gewh, gewh!*"

The king finally returned to his perch and stared at the Great Auk. "I should send you back to Neversink and let you explain why you've let this happen to your own colony. But you look too weak to swim that far, and I can't really spare the resources to haul you all the way back." Rozbell spoke as if the Great Auk had become nothing more than a terrible inconvenience. He turned to Feathertop and said, "Get this fossil out of my sight. I don't want to see him again. Oh, and that troublemaker who escaped. Find him and kill him too. As a sadistic tyrant, I do have a reputation to uphold!"

Feathertop swooped down and snatched the Great Auk's cage off its branch and hauled it into a clearing. Once Rozbell and Edmund were gone, too, Astra hurried out of the grove after Feathertop. The eagle had just pulled the Great Auk from his ripped-apart cage. "That puffin could have gotten pretty far by now," she said. "You'd better get going. I'll take care of this one."

Feathertop hesitated, disappointed to be deprived of a kill. But he agreed and took off, leaving the Great Auk with Astra.

The birds of Auk's Landing had a saying: "Nothing can hurt you on Neversink, except nature." This was an island that had burst up from the bottom of the ocean, created by the erupting lava of an undersea volcano. It had never been connected to any other landmass, and so there were no land mammals and no reptiles—in short, no natural predators.

Not all young survived, of course. Harsh weather claimed some. And yes, some seabirds, namely the sky roamers, were known to try and filch other birds' eggs from time to time. But Rozbell's fiendish new plan to harvest the auks' eggs meant disaster on a scale none of them could fathom.

Having seen the Great Auk's reaction, Rozbell wanted to tell the auks himself so that he could personally see an entire colony stricken with horror. So despite his annoyance at having to travel back and forth between the islands, he mounted an eagle owl to fly him over while Feathertop pursued Lockley, and when they landed, he stood on a high rock, visible to everyone, enjoying the effect of bright sunlight playing off his glittering gold crown.

Even before Rozbell started speaking, burrowing owls were invading auks' nests, rolling any eggs they found out into the open. Auks cried out in protest, but a fly-by from the formidable eagle owl backed them down.

"You're probably wondering what's going on," said Rozbell. "You see, I have arrived at a solution to the food shortage. For me, anyway."

An audible sense of horror spread through the crowd as

they realized what Rozbell was talking about. The pygmy king started cackling, and Egbert, who had been watching from the back, tried to use the distraction to sneak away to Lucy's burrow. As you can imagine, walruses generally find it difficult to sneak anywhere. Rozbell called out, "Not so fast, fatty!"

Egbert stopped, and when Rozbell flew over to him, he said as politely as possible, "I am not fat for an adult male walrus."

"A tooth-walker sensitive about his weight!" said Rozbell. "Well, that's just precious. Walk me to your place."

"Right now?" said Egbert, who was determined to get to Lucy's before the burrowing owls.

Rozbell's eyebrows nearly arched off the top of his head. "Yes, right now!"

Egbert reluctantly changed direction and led Rozbell to just north of Auk's Landing, where he had a rather messy nest littered with scrolls, scraps of sealskin and parchment decorated with both words and paintings, and the book prototype that he had unveiled at his party. Rozbell, who had mocked the book then, took a closer look now, kicking open the cover and roughly turning the pages with his foot. "I know you can read Owl, but I can't read Walrus," he said.

Egbert tried to hide his sense of superiority at this. Although owls were among the only bird species that could read and write, their written language technically wasn't Owl, but a hybrid bird language based on common song and speech patterns. Egbert had been able to pick up enough to learn to read it. Walrus, though, being the oldest written language, was largely symbolic and difficult to translate.

"The Scholars have never been interested in their work being widely accessible," said Egbert, sighing deeply as he said it.

"The Scholars?"

"It's difficult to explain," said Egbert.

"Oh well, then I've lost interest," said Rozbell, rummaging through some other scrolls. "What are these?"

"I'm working on a new book prototype in the birds' language. About Neversink!" said Egbert. He felt icky with Rozbell in his home, and yet his enthusiasm for literature made it hard for him to resist sharing with anyone who seemed interested.

"Yes, that's why I wanted to talk with you," Rozbell said silkily. "A project for you. An owl with my ambitions . . . I think someone should tell *his* story, don't you?"

"A history of an individual!" said Egbert. "I've often thought it was time for something like that," and he rummaged in his nest until he found a book he was working on: *I Am the Walrus: The Epic Adventures of the Universe's Most Avid Reader, Most Tireless Patron of the Arts, Most Honored Literary Critic, and All-Around Good Mammal.* "This is just the first of many planned volumes," he said, and showed Rozbell volume 1: *What an Autobiography Is and Why I Am the First Creature Ever to Write One.*

"Yes, fine," said Rozbell, losing a grip on his charm. "That's the idea, but more about *me.* Being king doesn't give me much spare time for writing."

"Oh," said Egbert. "Well, by definition, I can only write an autobiography about myself."

"Then make up a new word!" snapped Rozbell. He shut his eyes, feeling a tremor in his eyelids. Once he relaxed, he said, "This food shortage must be hard on a fellow your size. I may have an emergency stash of smidgens . . . perhaps extra nourishment would encourage you?"

"Oh, I could never take food from you," said Egbert. "Not with all that's going on. I may not be an auk, but Neversink is my home. And Lockley Puffin is my best friend."

"The troublemaker?" said Rozbell, whose bright eyes widened. Once again, Egbert had blundered into the sin of giving too much information, and it was obvious to Rozbell that Egbert thought Lockley was still in captivity. "Well, if you care about your friend, you'll accommodate me, like the rest of the colony." The king turned to go, then added, "I'll also be sending you some of my own work I'd like included in the book. Just some poems I've been jotting down over the years. They may need a touch of editing, but I think you'll find them as powerful as I do."

When Rozbell finally left, Egbert headed for Lucy's as quickly as possible. The burrowing owls would soon discover her, if they hadn't already. And even though Lucy hadn't laid her egg yet, it would be obvious she was pregnant, and they would come again. Maybe if he could get her to another location first, she and her egg would be safe.

He took the long way so as not to advertise where he was going, lurching over rocks and forcing himself through small passages to reach her. When he finally got there, he didn't bother knocking, instead thrusting his head through the front door. But it was Egbert who received a painful shock. For there was Lucy, standing over a solitary, grayish-white egg.

He stared at the egg and then at Lucy. "Move that into your bedroom," he said. "And don't come out of your burrow. Anyone who knows about you needs to think you're still pregnant!"

The urgency in his voice frightened Lucy. "Egbert, what's going on?"

"I can't explain right now," he said. "But here, I brought you something." And he unwrapped a small bundle of clams and oysters.

"Egbert!"

"You know and I know that auks don't store away food for the winter," he said. "But I do. Now eat something, regain your strength, and stay out of sight until I think of something."

DEATH ON THE MOORS, OR THE BITTERN'S LAMENT

When Lockley, Ruby, and the mole resurfaced, Lockley could tell they had gone sharply upland. The air was cool and damp. Coarse grasses grew in tufts and clumps around ponds of standing water. The ground beneath them was quilted with peat and embellished with the yellow and lavender buds of spiny gorse and flowering heather. Thickets of barbed thistles grew in abundance.

"Where are we, Mr. Mole?"

"North of the Midland Woods, as promised," the mole replied.

"That crazy badger said to stay off the moors," said Lockley, taking note of the surroundings. "Are moors anything like bogs?"

"They're exactly like bogs," said the mole. "You're familiar with such terrain?"

"We have a region on Neversink called the Black Bogs," Lockley explained. "This could be its twin."

Just then, Lockley's webbed foot sploshed into what felt like a slimy hole.

"Forgive me, Mr. Puffin," said the mole as he watched Lockley slowly sink into a thick soup of mud and decayed plant matter. His trembling voice was filled with genuine regret.

"Lockley!" said Ruby, zipping first next to him and then over to the mole. "What have you done?"

"I believe Mr. Mole has misled us," said Lockley with a sigh. "Tell me, was Otus in on it, or did you betray him too?"

"Oh no, poor Otus doesn't know," said the mole, wringing his paws. "I tried to explain, Mr. Puffin, we lesser creatures are at the beck and call of owls. And Rozbell's a frightful little thing. . . ."

"Wait a minute," said Ruby. "You mean the mole is a mole?"

Lockley felt the bog tugging at his legs, pulling him down. He vainly kicked his feet in hopes of gaining traction. "So you're just going to let me drown?"

"Oh no, I'm going to alert the northern owls that you're

trapped. Someone will fetch you. Assuming the Teeth of the Moors doesn't get here first."

"The what now?" said Ruby.

"I'm not a bad creature," the mole pleaded. "But no one wants to get eaten." He turned to go, but looked back briefly and said, "Don't kick. Kicking only makes it worse." And then he disappeared, leaving behind nothing but a small mound of dirt.

"Don't worry," said Ruby. "I'll save you." She began tugging at the scruff of Lockley's neck like a cat trying to carry off a kitten.

"Ow—ow! What are you doing? That's not going to work, Ruby!"

"It's no use," said Ruby, alighting on the spongy ground. "You're too fat."

"I am not fat for a puffin!" said Lockley, now sunk up to his waist. "Ruby, do something!"

"Wait!" said Ruby, who buzzed away excitedly. She returned with a long, slender branch, one end in her mouth and the other dragging on the ground.

"Brilliant!" said Lockley, but when he grabbed the free end and pulled, he nearly yanked Ruby into the bog with him.

"What are we gonna do?" said Ruby. As small as her face was, it still betrayed her sense of panic.

"Maybe there's time to find help," said Lockley, without

much confidence. The bog was gurgling just below his neck.

Ruby rose up above the tussocks and looked out over the bleak moorland in all directions.

"What do you see?"

She spun around a few more times before answering. "Nothing." But then, "What's that?" And like a flame being snuffed, Ruby was gone, trailing smoke behind her. When she returned, almost as quickly, she asked, "Did you hear that?"

"Hear what?" said Lockley, his voice filled with panic. But then, he did hear it. The low, booming notes of the legendary moorbird known as the bittern.

Suddenly a mad, clucking cry erupted from the heather, and a reddish-brown rocket propelled itself straight up with fast-whirring wingbeats, screeching, "*Go back, go back, go back*" in rapid succession. Ruby bolted straight up, and the frenetic attacker fell to earth into a clump of grass near Lockley.

"Cedric!" came a female voice, and Lockley saw a strange pair of birds approach: one that looked like a blue-and-green chicken, and another with stiltlike legs and a spear for a bill.

"Oh my goodness," said the chicken bird, her head jerking back and forth.

"Please, help me," said Lockley.

"Cedric, Bruce!" she called, and the stilt-legged bird skittered closer, joined by a bird with a short, broad tail and small, hooked beak. "Help me pull this poor thing out."

"Yeah, hurry!" said Ruby, who was eye level again.

The bog was almost up to Lockley's bill, and the two male birds weren't too happy about having to get their wings dirty. But the three strangers finally managed to pull Lockley out with a great *suck*. He was left lying on his back, covered in mud.

"What is it, Cedric?" whispered the chicken bird. "It looks like a duck with a pet horsefly."

"Little one's a hummingbird," said Cedric. "But the other one . . ."

"Here we go," muttered Lockley.

"Look at the fruity bill," said the stilt-legged bird. "It's obviously a parrot, or a macaw."

"Those birds live in the tropics," said Ruby.

"So do hummingbirds," said Cedric. "And yet, here you are."

For once, Ruby was speechless.

"What about the shapeless body?" said the chicken bird. "It could be a dodo. Or a small emu."

"I can fly," said Lockley, who was now up, shaking mud from his feathers.

"A harlequin duck? A barnacle goose? A loon? A scaup? A coot?"

Lockley began tapping his foot peevishly.

"A tapir."

"An eggplant."

"One of those isn't a bird," said Lockley, "and the last one isn't even an animal! I'm a puffin, for crying out loud! Lockley J. Puffin, of the Neversink puffins!"

"Puffin!" said Cedric. "You're a wanted bird!"

"I gathered," said Lockley.

"Agnes, Bruce—help me push him back in."

"What? No!" Lockley backed away while trying not to step into another bog, and Ruby flew at Cedric, spoiling for a fight.

"Stop it right now!" said the chicken bird, her head jerking back and forth. "How rude of us. I'm Agnes Moorhen. This is Cedric Grouse," she said, pointing to the gruff bird with the hooked beak. "And this is Bruce Bittern." The stilt-legged bird bobbed his head up and down.

"You're the legendary bittern?" said Lockley, gawking at the small bird with the booming voice.

"He gets that all the time," Cedric scoffed.

Lockley shook the last of the mud off his feet. "As I said, I'm Lockley Puffin, and this is my friend Ruby."

Ruby did a midair bow.

"Why did you want to push me back in?" said Lockley. "Are the moorbirds are in cahoots with Rozbell?"

"Rozbell?" Cedric asked.

"Yeah, Rozbell," said Ruby. "Tiny owl with a Napoleon complex?"

The moorhen, the bittern, and the grouse all looked at one another quizzically.

"Never mind her," said Lockley. "She comes from a different world entirely."

"We know who Rozbell is," said the grouse. "And no, we do not *cahoot* with him. But owls are looking for you, and if we're seen together, he'll tar and defeather us all."

"Cedric," said Agnes, "there's no reason to be rude. Mr. Puffin, if I may ask, how did you end up here?"

Lockley proceeded to explain what had befallen Neversink, how he and the Great Auk were captured, how Ruby had sprung him, and how the mole had tricked them.

"Those owls," said Agnes, clucking her tongue.

Cedric agreed. "I've always said, power corrupts. But *owlbsolute* power corrupts *owlbsolutely*."

"I've never heard you say that," said Bruce.

Cedric ignored him. "The Roundheads—that's what owls who wear hats call themselves—they've revived an old plan to drain the moors and marshes."

"Why would they do that?" Lockley wondered.

"To plant more trees! They want to develop all this into forest!" said Cedric, spreading his wings toward the gray, flat horizon. "Connect the Midland Woods with the Great Northern Forest to the north. One big owl roosting territory from the downlands to the highlands!"

"So you'd have to move," said Lockley.

"Move? Perish is more like it," snapped the grouse. "The vegetation we eat, the insects and the frogs—all wetland species. We can't just up and move every time an owl wants our spot!"

"I know what you mean," said Lockley.

"Boy, owls sure do hate birds who like water!" said Ruby.

Bruce Bittern's neck stretched up in alarm. "The fog is creeping in!" He punctuated the thought with three eerie, booming bass notes. Indeed, as darkness slowly absorbed the light and the air cooled, cottony strands of fog began to unspool over the ground.

"Mr. Puffin, you and your friend might want to get off the moors soon," said Agnes.

"The Teeth of the Moors?" Lockley asked.

"You've heard of him?"

"Only recently."

Agnes began jerking her head back and forth and twitching in circles again. "He prowls the moors at night looking for animals trapped in the bogs or wandering about. We all have our hiding places, but oh dear, Mr. Puffin, you rather stick out like a will-o'-the-wisp."

Lockley began extending and folding his right wing gingerly. "I'm not sure I can fly at the moment," he said. "I think you hurt my shoulder when you pulled me out."

"You're welcome," Cedric replied tartly.

Just then they heard the first fearful, guttural rumblings coming from the bowels of the fog. They all looked at one another, silent for a moment.

"Can you really not fly?" said Agnes, twitching all over with worry.

"I'm not sure." Lockley spread his wings, flinching in pain, and then took a small running start and got himself airborne. His weakened right side caused him to fly in a wobbly, lopsided circle, coming closer and closer to the ground, until . . . "Not again," he cried, just before splatting into another bog.

Ruby flew to him, followed by Agnes, muttering, "Oh dear, oh dear," over and over.

"Get over here this instant!" screamed Agnes at the grouse and the bittern. They obeyed, and once again Lockley found himself being pulled from the clammy grasp of the earth and laid muddy on his back.

"It's useless," he moaned. "I'm not a puffin, I'm a sitting duck!"

"A sitting duck!" said Agnes. "That gives me an idea. Mr. Puffin, pluck me out some of your feathers!"

No matter how much Lockley wanted to escape the Teeth of the Moors, he wasn't at all happy with what followed. The moorhen led them to a marsh-mallow patch, where the squishy white fruit of the marsh-mallow plant grew in abundance. She picked one, attached Lockley's feathers to it, added a carrot nose, and set it back in the bog.

"A decoy!" said Ruby.

"Why does the decoy have to look like me?" said Lockley. "And a *carrot*?"

"Would you rather look like a carrot or be chomped like one?" said Cedric.

"You do have a white belly," said the bittern. "And it's a little on the squidgy side."

"Besides," said Cedric, "we can all fly away. You're the one endangering us."

The remark was intended to be flippant, but Lockley felt it deeply. It seemed to sum up his entire efforts to fight the owls. "You're right," he said. "The only way for me to escape the Teeth of the Moors is to defeat the Teeth of the Moors. I should be thanking you."

Cedric stared at him.

"Thank you," said Lockley.

The grouse snorted, and then the three moorbirds, Lockley, and Ruby all hid behind a mossy rock. *Here goes nothing*, Lockley thought. "Help! Help! I appear to be hopelessly stuck," he yelled, and then they waited.

Before long the hellish rumblings crept nearer. Lockley imagined the billowing fog to be puffs of hot breath from the nostrils of this unseen beast. As dusk settled over them,

Lockley could hear the distant hoots and calls of the northerly woodland owls—the long-eared owl, the hawk owl, the eagle owl, and the tawny—and he felt sure they were transmitting the mole's intelligence back to Rozbell. But he didn't have time to stew over it. For across a tussock and through the mist came a prowling beast, measuring the ground with impossibly long legs and fiery yellow eyes. Its bearded head swung low, six-inch-long canines overhung a drooling jaw, and from its gullet came that awful death rattle. It made straight for the decoy.

The ferocity with which its jaws snapped up the decoy puffin made Lockley jump. But the trap worked to perfection. The beast quickly discovered the futility of trying to chew a ripe marsh-mallow. White goop stuck to its teeth and oozed out of its mouth, and the powerful jaws struggled to open as if the top and bottom were held together with rubber bands. The death rattle turned to a frustrated whimper as its whole body writhed in the struggle against the sticky surprise. Turning and twisting, the beast trod backward, heedless of everything except the goop, until its hind legs plunged into the bog. The fire in its eyes went out, replaced by fear, and struggling only mired the beast more deeply. Lockley and Ruby watched dumbstruck as the predator eventually sank to its neck, seeming to foam at the mouth with white mallow, black feathers sticking to its nose and chin.

When they were sure the beast was vanquished, Lockley stumbled into a sitting position, his eyes wide. "I hate the moors," he said softly.

"Lockley, we have to keep going," said Ruby. "Lucy needs you, and the owls are bound to be on to us by now."

Lockley stood up and tried his wing again, grimacing as he extended and folded it. Agnes suggested they could all do with a bit of nourishment, which reminded Lockley of what had started all this. "Are none of you afraid to eat because of the Sickness?" he asked. "Or perhaps the rumors are to your advantage? If your normal predators are afraid to eat you?"

"Pshaw," groused Cedric. "It's no comfort if the plague starts even lower on the food chain."

"How low?" said Ruby, who plunged low enough to hover just above the grouse's tiny head.

"All of the creatures who have supposedly died because of the Sickness—small birds and rodents in particular—eat insects, or host them as parasites. I eat mostly vegetation, but some insects. Agnes and Bruce here both eat frogs and such, which eat insects. You get the idea. We're all doomed."

"Cedric!" said Agnes.

Ruby began coughing and choking and trying to spit out the imaginary wad of food in her mouth. "Lockley! I inhaled a whole tunnelful of insects with that mole!"

"Calm down," said Lockley. "It's just a theory. There's

nothing to worry about."

"I wouldn't say that," said Cedric.

"I think I'm going to be sick," said Ruby.

"Poor dear," said Agnes, her head and tail twitching. And then: "That's it! Be sick!"

"Mission accomplished," said Ruby.

"No, I mean—wait right there," and she darted off on her chicken legs, only to return a few minutes later with a leafy plant clutched in her bill.

"You can't possibly believe I'm hungry *now*," said Ruby.

"Trust me—just eat," scolded the moorhen, and so Ruby reluctantly began to nibble on the harmless-looking leaves. It took only a few seconds for their purpose to become clear. Ruby began turning shades of green and purple and wobbling in midair like a butterfly caught in a crosswind. Suddenly she began shaking violently, her whole tiny body convulsing. And then, it happened—she puked. Right at Lockley's feet, to be precise. Lockley couldn't believe so much vomit could come out of one little bird, but there it was.

"Lovely," he said.

"Boy, do I feel better," said Ruby.

"I wish I could say the same," said Lockley, shaking small chunks off his feet.

Agnes came to Lockley bearing strange plants with orange flowers. "I brought something for you, too, Mr. Puffin."

He shook his head. "The last thing I ate was fish, on Neversink. I don't need to bring it back up."

"Just hold still," said Agnes, and she began chewing the flowers into a balm, which she applied to Lockley's wounded shoulder. "You're going to need to be stronger to fly home."

"That does feel good," said Lockley.

"What now?" said Ruby.

"Well, old girl, if the owls know we're here, we don't have much choice but to fly away as fast as we can." Turning to Agnes, he asked, "Any suggestions?"

"Let me think," and she began scratching at the dirt with her feet. "We're *here*, between the two great forests. On the western coast, to the north, is the Bay of Whales, *here*. I know it doesn't make sense, but I would stay out in the open. Auks fly near the water's surface, don't they?" Lockley nodded. "Good, you can keep close to the ground and fly across the meadows, using the tall grasses for cover. Follow this route," she added, scratching a diagonal line northwest from the moors to the bay. "However, I suggest you let us keep you overnight. The owls will be coming out to hunt now, and your injured wing could use the rest."

Lockley thanked Agnes, while Cedric and Bruce just grunted and encouraged them to be gone already. The next morning, the moorbirds watched as Lockley and Ruby shrank along the horizon, then shuffled off. And in leaving, they all missed the sight of a dark, hawklike bird, sailing with flat, swept-back wings over the moors, landing by the bog where the Teeth of the Moors had vanished, and retrieving a mouthful of Lockley's plucked feathers.

THIS IS GOOD-BYE

Once Lockley and Ruby were off the moors, the land spread before them in a rolling expanse of tall grasses and flowering plants. Lockley was used to vast horizons, but here the wrinkled gray sea and toothy glaciers of his world were replaced by gentle waves of limestone hills and fertile meadows of snowdrops, daffodils, buttercups, and cowslips that teemed with color like a coral reef.

Following Agnes's advice, they picked up the river, which flowed down into the countryside from a mountainous spine the natives called the Backbone. Lockley, for once grateful for his low, charging style of flight, kept just below the tops of the tallest grasses while Ruby followed close behind.

Flying near to the ground, though, Lockley saw something that contradicted the sweeping beauty of his surroundings: dead birds and rodents, whose carcasses normally would have been carried off by predators or picked clean by scavengers, left rotting and crawling with insects. And once, Lockley glimpsed a jarring sight in the distance above the grass line. It appeared to be a large bird of prey—possibly a hawk—struggling to perch on the slender branches of a bush as he used his meat-eating beak to strip it of leaves and berries.

Near midday they stopped to rest and drink from the river before concealing themselves in the grass again.

"I know I don't live here, but it's obvious things aren't right," said Lockley as they discussed the odd and disturbing images.

"Yeah, something's fishy all right," said Ruby.

"No, *fishy* is good," said Lockley. "Something's *owly.* As that malevolent mole said, whether the Sickness has returned or not, Rozbell has the beasts of Tytonia believing it. Either that, or they're just afraid to defy him by eating their normal diet."

"Speaking of eating . . . are you okay?" said Ruby. She hadn't dared inhale another insect, despite their abundance. But she had sipped nectar among the many flowers along the way. Lockley, though, hadn't eaten a solid meal since being kidnapped. He'd been given only water in captivity, and Agnes had only gotten him to eat some leafy greens.

"I'm okay," said Lockley. Like many birds, he could go stretches without food, though he did feel weaker, and despite Agnes's balm, his wing was still sore. But there was an ache inside him that wasn't from a lack of food. He had been thinking of all that had happened and all they had seen—the extinct badger kingdom and the moorbirds threatened with removal, the other creatures forced to alter their way of life—and he thought of the Great Auk's last words to him. *The spirit journey is not for the faint of heart. You could take Lucy elsewhere.* The Great Auk was giving him an out. *Leadership is an unfair burden.*

Lockley sat there watching Ruby sample flower after flower, oblivious to the world around her. She finally noticed that Lockley was staring at her. "What's up, L? You don't look well."

"Ruby, when we get to the sea, I need you to head directly to Neversink."

"Well, *duh,*" she said. "With you right behind me. Right? Lockley?" She alighted on the ground at his feet.

"I do plan to return to Neversink," said Lockley. "After I go to Ocean's End."

Ruby was instantly airborne again, abuzz. "Are you crazy, Lockley?"

"I have to, Ruby. The Great Auk told Rozbell that it may be preferable to perish than to live as an owl's slave. Maybe so. But even better is to live as an independent auk. A *colony* of independent auks." He paused for a moment. "Besides, I made things worse—with Sedna, I mean. I *should* be the one to make the spirit journey."

"What's the spirit journey?" Ruby asked.

"It's how we appease Sedna. It's how we bring the food back to Neversink. Beyond that, I'm not entirely sure," Lockley admitted. "But I will figure it out. I have to."

"That's great," said Ruby. "But you don't need to go it alone. I'll come with you! I've helped so far!"

"You certainly have," said Lockley. "But I need you to go home and tell Egbert and Lucy I'm okay, and that I'll be back. Help Egbert take care of Lucy." When Ruby looked at him doubtfully, he said, "At least help protect Lucy from Egbert!"

"Now you're talking sense," said Ruby, and they took to the air again with new resolve. To the east was a deep, dark forest of towering trees the likes of which Lockley had never seen. Giant coniferous pine, juniper, fir, and spruce peaked above rowan, oak, and alder, silver birch, beech, and willow. He was far enough away to admire just how large the forest was. Looking at the colossal trunks and lofty canopies of leaves supported by sturdy outstretched wooden arms, he felt slightly jealous of the perching birds. It seemed so grand and so safe way up there. Part of him wondered how the first Great Auk of the World Tree could have abandoned such a fine home.

"That must be the Great Northern Forest," said Lockley. "It rather puts the Midland Woods to shame, don't you think?"

"You should see the jungle," said Ruby. "Nothing but huge trees from coast to coast. Of course, all trees look big to me."

Before long it was clear they had reached the highlands. Wild tufts of grass were bent low by strong winds and framed by rough ridges of sandstone and granite. Long-horned cattle and goats grazed the open spaces. The air was cool and dry. Both Lockley and Ruby could smell the briny Northern Sea in the wind gusts.

If you studied the map at the front of this book (and if you didn't, you really should), you will have noticed that Tytonia grows narrow at its northernmost point, and the Bay of Whales, their intended destination, is like a small mouth on the northwestern coast.

When he smelled the familiar air, Lockley veered due north from the river to a granite outcropping that dropped steeply off to the sea. To the north were hundreds of small rock islands, jutting out of the water, covered with moss and lichens and battered with sea spray. The auks used to call these the Crab-Back Islands. Lockley grew still and quiet and breathed it all in deeply. "Ruby, do you know where we are?"

"I know where we're not. We're not on the moors. And

we're not on Neversink. . . . Lockley, let's go!"

"We're on Murre Mountain," he said, standing at the precipice, above all those nooks and crannies so favored by the auks. He could almost hear the deep, hoarse *arrrs* of a thriving murre colony drifting up the cliff face. Lockley continued to stand there, silent and proud as he overlooked his ancestral home, where the first Great Auk had roosted after he left the World Tree.

"Lockley!" said Ruby. "Turn around!"

"What?" Lockley turned back toward the highlands. Behind them a large bird soared in their direction. Its silhouette was unmistakably that of an eagle.

"Feathertop!" Lockley's first reaction was to head for the river, where he could submerge himself and try to swim away. But he needed a running start to get airborne, and if you've ever seen a duck or a goose run, you know that short, webbed feet aren't made for sprinting. Feathertop banked to the west to cut him off.

"You'll never make it, Lockley!" cried Ruby. And then to Lockley's horror, the tiny hummingbird flew straight at the eagle, as if she believed she could knock him out of the air.

"Ruby, no!" Lockley took flight, ignoring the lingering ache in his right wing, and then veered away from the river, toward Feathertop.

The martial eagle had never had his prey fly directly

at him before. As the two birds approached him, he stuck out first one talon, then the other, losing his balance in the twisting highland winds. He tried to brake with his wings, but it was too late . . . the eagle plummeted toward the earth, nearly goring himself on a bull's long horn.

As Feathertop rolled along the ground, Lockley veered back toward Murre Mountain. "Ruby, if you had any doubts about splitting up, do it now! He can't catch both of us!"

"No!" said Ruby. "We can take him! Get up, Featherbrain!"

"Ruby! Get to Neversink!"

Lockley didn't wait for her to argue. He beat his wings furiously for the Northern Sea, the granite peaks racing toward him, until the precipice of Murre Mountain was beneath him. He took one look over his shoulder and saw that Feathertop was airborne again and bearing down on him, and then he tucked his wings and plunged down the cliff side, disappearing into the white spray of the violent sea just as Feathertop swept overhead.

Egbert's new job as Rozbell's official editor and biographer (a word they still hadn't invented) threatened to do him in. The king's poems—long, epic verses—were actually part of one even longer cycle, entitled *Song of Rozbell: Warrior-Poet.* In the short history of literature at this point, Rozbell's poetry was probably the worst stuff ever written. In fact, for eons afterward, dictator poetry was regarded as the most deplorable trend in publishing until the dawn of celebrity children's books.

The sheer volume of the material Rozbell had sent to Egbert made it difficult for him to be as vigilant as he needed to be for Lucy. A small crew of burrowing owls was on Neversink almost every day now, checking and double-checking nests for any eggs they had missed or that had just been laid. Egbert had hoped that successfully shielding Lucy's burrow a few times would be enough, that the owls would quit looking down at her end. But auk nests are so close together that there was a constant danger of them stumbling onto Lucy's by accident.

Finally Egbert remembered all the times Lockley had used Arne Puffin and other immature birds as distractions, and so he called a group of them together.

"What do you say to a game to take our minds off our hunger?" said Egbert. "*Not* Pin the Sea Urchin on the Walrus," he added quickly when he saw their faces light up. "I thought we could try something new."

"Wait," said Snorri Guillemot. "This isn't going to be like that time Lockley made us *work*, is it?" The others groaned.

"Oh, no!" said Egbert. "I thought we could have a little fun with, you know, *the owls*," he whispered. They seemed skeptical. It was one thing to pick on Egbert, but the owls? "I've got some special treats for anyone who helps me out."

He held out two finfuls of small fish. The young auks' bills dropped.

"Where did you get that?" said Arne Puffin.

"Never mind," said Egbert. "But believe me, it wasn't easy. Which shows you how important this is to me."

Egbert told them his plan, and from that point forward, when any burrowing owls came near Lucy's burrow, the young auks would immediately circle them, herding them elsewhere by swearing they had seen eggs in another part of the colony, or that Astra had asked to see them, or whatever else their imaginative young minds could come up with.

Their assistance took a load off Egbert, and he congratulated himself on his ingenuity. But just when he thought he had less to worry about, Egbert received an unexpected summons. Neversink's Council of Elders wanted to see him.

Egbert remembered hearing the term from the Great Auk once when he was talking to him about the colony's history. Though the Great Auk was the law-speaker, in theory there was a Council of Elders, made up of one senior bird from each species, who could be called upon to resolve minor conflicts, vote on any proposed changes in the colony's day-to-day affairs, or—in the absence of a law-speaker—govern the colony. As you already know if you've been reading up to now (and if you haven't been reading up to now, why are you starting here?), auks don't typically have a lot of affairs to deal with. The last time the Council met was to decide who should be on the Council.

When Egbert arrived at the meeting place, he was met by Algard Guillemot, Tor Razorbill, Egil Murre, and a barely conscious puffin named Grimsey.

"So this is the Council of Elders," said Egbert.

"We're not sure," Algard admitted. "It's been so long since we elected it. In any event, this is who's here now."

Egbert resisted a strong urge to tout the benefits of being able to write things down.

"I'll come right to the point," said Algard. "We've decided to ask you to leave."

"But I just got here!"

"Not this meeting, Egbert. We're asking you to leave Neversink."

Egbert snorted. "Don't be absurd. I have to be here when Lockley returns. And in the meantime, Lucy needs me."

Algard looked at the others as if to say, *I told you getting rid of a four-thousand-pound mammal wouldn't be easy.* "Yes, Lucy," he said. "It has come to our attention that you have been hoarding food."

Egbert pinkened a little. "I think *hoarding* is a bit of an exaggeration," he blustered. "I had some extra, and poor Lucy needed nourishment. If you could have seen her right after Lockley was taken—"

"Egbert," said Algard, cutting him off, "where did you get stores of food?"

Egil Murre lunged forward, pointing at Egbert. "He's working for the owls!"

"What? I am not!"

"We see you with Rozbell!" said Tor Razorbill.

"Oh, that," said Egbert. "He's making me edit his poetry. For the love of Sedna, it almost makes me wish I couldn't read!"

"Egbert!" said Algard, more forcefully this time. "Whether you're getting food from the owls or hoarding old catches, you have betrayed us. Any stores of food should have been shared with the entire colony, not given to one puffin."

"It was hardly enough to feed the colony," said Egbert. "And I didn't give it all to Lucy. Just enough to revive her. And I'm a walrus! You must understand I need more than any of you!"

"Precisely," said Algard. "You have been living among *our* colony, fishing *our* waters. And until this crisis is resolved, we can't allow a beast with your appetite consuming what few stray portions of food remain."

"What are you saying?" said Egbert, his whiskers vibrating.

"I already told you. We took a vote and decided you have to go." The other Elders nodded, except Grimsey, who had fallen asleep. Algard kept his eyes on Egbert's until the crestfallen walrus dropped his head and turned away.

Egbert was devastated. He slouched back to his nest and began to gather a few of his things, including his favorite books—all written by himself. He thought about how he had failed his friends, and how he would be unable to help Lucy now. And the young auks would tire of their new game soon, especially with no food to offer as bribes. What would Lockley find when he returned?

Lockley! thought Egbert. He realized he might never see his best friend again. Or Lucy. He even felt an ache that he might have bantered with Ruby for the last time. He left his things and made the long slog back to Lucy's to tell her.

As soon as he did, Lucy ignored all his warnings about being seen in public and marched straight to Algard's.

"Lockley was right. You're nothing but a coward!" she said. Her tone caught him off guard. "You won't stand up for yourself or your colony against the owls, but you'll stand up to poor Egbert!"

If you've gotten the impression that Algard was heartless in addition to being crusty, you may have been misled, somewhat. Part of him actually felt bad about what he did to Egbert. Lucy's words stung. And she wasn't done.

"You accuse Egbert of working with the owls? As soon as the Great Auk's out of the picture, you dig up the so-called Council of Elders. Is that even real? Maybe we should be wondering if *you're* part of the owl takeover!"

"Lucy! How dare you!"

"How dare *you*, Algard." And she stormed back to her burrow, leaving the guillemot with his red tongue hanging from his bill.

When the time came for Egbert to leave, Lucy walked him down to the water's edge to see him off. "I guess this is good-bye," he said wearily.

Lucy launched into the unfairness of it all and promised Egbert that Lockley and the Great Auk would make sure he was brought back once they returned. She was being strong for Egbert, but he could see the fear in her eyes. He was being exiled, but she was being abandoned. And he knew the thought had crossed her mind more than once that Lockley might never return.

Egbert lowered his enormous head and put his face as close to Lucy as he could. "Lockley is the scrappiest puffin I've ever met," he said. "There is no doubt in my mind he's just fine. You won't be alone for long."

To Egbert's surprise, Lucy grabbed his whiskers with her wing tips and gently rubbed her bill against his rough cheek. The gesture almost made Egbert burst into tears, which probably would have drowned poor Lucy. But he regained his composure and straightened back up. Then Egbert took up his things and paddled into the surf, slowly disappearing from view as the waves closed over him.

PART THREE
Ocean's End

VOYAGE OF THE SHUNNED

Lockley sank so fast once he hit the water that he scraped bottom. It was sheer luck, he knew, that he didn't shatter himself on some submerged rock. He quickly righted himself underwater and began flying in earnest through the current. His goal was to use the Crab-Backs for cover, but when he finally resurfaced, he realized to his horror that a riptide had pulled him into open water.

In a matter of moments, a formidable shadow rippled through the waves. Lockley just had time to catch his breath and dive again as Feathertop struck at the sea. Lockley felt the spear-like talons on his back as the eagle tried to fish him out of the water, but the grip was weak, and he wriggled free. The effort kept Lockley from diving far, though, and as he bobbed to the surface again, he saw Feathertop circling back for another attack.

Lockley turned toward the Crab-Backs, determined to make it there on his next dive. He glanced again at Feathertop, who was now picking up frightening speed. As soon as the eagle tucked his wings to dive, Lockley dove away from the surface, praying to Sedna that his timing was true. Feathertop crashed into the waves, losing his balance when he grabbed nothing but water, and Lockley seized the advantage. He tunneled his way through the currents, leaving the surface and Feathertop's fearful weapons far behind. After a long descent, he veered away from Murre Mountain and aimed again for the small islands, hoping to resurface and take cover somewhere in the outer ring.

Most of the Crab-Backs are hardly more than oversized stepping stones, as if the gods had laid themselves a footpath from the tip of Tytonia to the Arctic Circle. A few, though, are of considerable size, and so honeycombed through the ages by wind and ocean waves that they offer an ideal place of refuge. It was inside one of these dank, dark caves that Lockley finally found sanctuary, squirting out of the sea into the mouth of a large igneous rock and collapsing from exhaustion.

The next morning, Lockley's injured wing was aflame with pain again, and poking his head out of the cave, he thought he saw Feathertop's silhouette against the sun. *There's no way he could search every rock,* thought Lockley, but there was a reason eagles were such good hunters, and Lockley was afraid of making the slightest movement out in the open as long as Feathertop was still looking for him. That made fishing out of the question, and Lockley had already been without solid food for days. Hungry and weakened, he lay down to rest his sore wing, and as the sun again approached the horizon, he began to despair.

During his fitful half sleep, Lockley thought he saw the Great Auk, still caged, swinging above him, looking down on him with pity. Later in the night, an even more disturbing image floated before him: Lucy, feather-bare, serving Rozbell a tray of smidgens with her own egg as the centerpiece. He came awake, shivering. The cold spray of the Northern Sea was splashing through the mouth of the cave, and Lockley was drenched.

Struggling to his feet, Lockley decided then and there he would not end up as food for scavengers on some nameless rock. He couldn't fly yet, but he could try to find something to eat. He searched the cave walls and found what looked like wet snot—slimy green splotches of algae—and began licking it for nourishment. It tasted like wet snot, too, but the nutrient-rich plant did give him some strength back. The only problem was, he began to hallucinate. In addition to the phantom images of the Great Auk and Lucy that had visited his sleep, he swore that he was now hearing the ghostly cries of Egbert, calling to him across the waves.

Oh, woe is me! came the wailing walrus voice. *Woe, woe is me. . . .*

That's just like Egbert, thought a delusional Lockley, *to call attention to himself even as a figment of my imagination.*

Lockley went to the opening, convinced that being in the cave's dark cavity was causing him to lose his mind. When he saw no sign of Feathertop, he sat down at the water's edge to drink in the fresh air. He watched the waves lap the rocks, over and over, and he thought again of the Great Auk. Lockley grasped the clamshell necklace he had been given, feathering it gently, trying not to imagine what Rozbell had done to him. And then, Lockley thought he heard something—something between a sigh and a sob, echoing among the Crab-Backs. It was hard to tell where it was coming from exactly, until the mournful creature finally exclaimed, "Oh, woe is me!"

It can't be, thought Lockley. That was *not* his imagination. He plunged into the water and swam in the direction of the voice, and when he squirted back out of the sea onto a large open rock, he couldn't believe his eyes.

"Egbert!"

"Lockley!"

Lockley had never been so happy to see his large friend. He would have given him a hug, except that it is physically impossible for a puffin and a walrus to embrace. As for Egbert, when he actually set eyes on his clown-colored little mate, his emotions got the best of him. Great tears rolled off his face like a waterfall. Were it not for his webbed feet, Lockley would have been swept off the rock in a river of joy.

"Did you come looking for me, Egbert?"

Egbert patted his eyes dry with his fins. "Not exactly. Oh, my dear Lockley, it's terrible . . . just terrible. . . ."

"There, there, old boy," said Lockley. "Take your time."

"Poor Lucy," blubbered Egbert. The mention of her name made Lockley's heart spasm, but Egbert choked up before he could finish.

"What about Lucy? Egbert, she's all right, isn't she?"

You can forgive Lockley, after all he had been through, for expecting a short, straight answer out of a walrus, especially to such an important question. Egbert proceeded to tell him, with great drama, all that had happened since Lockley's kidnapping, leaving out very little detail. A frantic Lockley finally learned that Lucy was alive and well when Egbert left, and then Egbert admitted that he had been banished from Neversink, and he told Lockley why. "Can you imagine?" said Egbert, still indignant. "Me, in cahoots with owls?"

For his part, Lockley was moved almost to tears that Egbert had put himself at such risk to protect Lucy. He felt ashamed, too, wondering if despite the promises he had made to himself, he had done as much as Egbert to protect her. "You're a brave soul," said Lockley, patting Egbert's leathery hide. "But Egbert, what are you doing on the Crab-Backs? You said you didn't come looking for me, so why did you travel south instead of returning to your clan at Ocean's End?"

Egbert reddened a bit. "Lockley . . . there's something I've never told you."

"Really?" said Lockley. The idea of Egbert keeping quiet about anything was astonishing. "Come on, Egbert, you can tell me."

Egbert looked him straight in the eye. "I was Shunned."

"Beg your pardon?"

"I didn't leave Ocean's End of my own accord. I was a Scholars' apprentice, but the Scholars objected to my ideas about spreading the written word to, um, *lesser* creatures."

"I see," Lockley replied stiffly. He wasn't sure why he was so offended, since he had never expressed any desire to let Egbert teach him to read or write.

"They thought my ideas were dangerous," Egbert continued. "So they administered the Shunning."

"I'm guessing that's bad?"

"Lockley, nothing is worse than being Shunned! It means I can never return to my clan again!"

Lockley realized for the first time that Egbert had not come to Neversink as an ambassador for the written word.

He had just been looking for a new home.

"Lockley, there's something else I haven't told you." Screwing up his courage, Egbert then explained Rozbell's ghastly new plan for feeding himself. Lockley was so horror-struck that Egbert was afraid to reveal the one other important detail he had left out. But he knew he must, and so he gave Lockley the bittersweet news: Lucy had laid her egg. An egg that was now in mortal danger.

Lockley had to sit down again. Egbert joined him at the edge of the rock. "Well, that's that, then, isn't it?" Lockley said quietly.

"What do you mean?"

Lockley didn't explain at first, still turning things over in his mind. "I wasn't on my way back to Neversink, Egbert. I was headed to Ocean's End. The Great Auk . . . it's hard to explain, but I was going to try to make the spirit journey, to see Sedna. I sent Ruby back to help you watch over Lucy."

"Well, you can't worry about that now," said Egbert. "Lucy needs you. Even assuming Ruby made it back, the only thing standing between Lucy and those burrowing owls would be a hummingbird! A very aggressive, aggravating hummingbird, I grant you. But still!"

Lockley fell silent again. He had never felt so conflicted.

"Lockley, what is it?" said Egbert.

"I . . . I can't go back to Neversink, Egbert. Not yet."

"But, Lockley—Lucy's egg! *Your* egg!"

Lockley just shook his head. "Even if I could protect my own egg from the owls, where would that leave us? Still starving. The Great Auk told me how to save the colony, and it's up to me to do it. *Me*," said Lockley, as if he didn't quite believe it himself.

Egbert was stunned. He loved Lockley, but he never would have expected him to attempt a journey of this sort. "Are you sure about this, my dear?"

Lockley nodded firmly. "I am."

"Then I think I can help." When Lockley looked at him hopefully, Egbert said, "There's a chance the story of Sedna is written somewhere in the library of the Scholars, at Ocean's End."

"The walrus scholars, of course!" said Lockley. "You think they might know 'The Tricking of Sedna'? And how we might be able to find her?"

"Some version, anyway," said Egbert. "At least, a *written* version."

"But Egbert, how would we get in? You just told me you were shunned, and I hardly think they'd let a puffin in, even if I could read."

Egbert stroked his whiskers and closed his eyes. When he opened them again, he looked straight at Lockley. "Well, my dear, we'll just have to find a way, won't we? This is too important not to try." Even as he said this, he could see doubt in Lockley's face. "Lucy has twice the backbone of your average auk," Egbert assured him. "She can take care of herself. You're doing exactly what the Great Auk would do. And what's more, *I'm* going to help you do it."

Lockley smiled and grabbed Egbert's whiskers.

"Why does everyone want to do that?" said Egbert, grooming them back into place.

"I don't know what I'd do without you, old boy," said Lockley. "You and me, an unstoppable force, right?" And so with good spirits but great trepidation, they set off for the north, to Ocean's End.

Lockley was so tired from the flight that his feathers felt like lead, and he crashed onto the Arctic ice with even less grace than usual. Moments later Egbert's head popped out of the slushy water. He plopped his fins facedown on the edge of the ice shelf, like a child peering onto a table, and then speared the ice with his tusks to help haul himself out of the sea. (If you remember that Rozbell derisively referred to walruses as tooth-walkers, now you know why.)

After a brief rest, they plunged back into the water to feed, for they were both famished after their long trip. For Egbert especially, it was a relief to be back in food-rich waters. Lockley was relieved at how much better his wing felt—perhaps the icy water had some healing effect—but he returned sooner than he had planned after hearing some loud, strange sounds below.

"Did you hear it, Egbert?" he whispered. "Like a thumping, or a pounding, following by a ringing!" In fact, if you were to hear it yourself, you might say it sounded like a carpenter hammering a nail into a board until a kitchen timer went off.

"Of course I heard it—those are walruses." He could see the puzzled look on Lockley's face. "You know, I thought auks sounded funny the first time I heard them too." And he proceeded to do his best impression of a growling murre or a hissing guillemot.

"Sorry," said Lockley, gesturing toward the sound, "but I've never heard *you* sound quite like that."

"That's because those are males and females communicating," Egbert explained. "It's breeding season here, too. You might say those are love poems."

"I don't think I'd like poetry," said Lockley.

To Lockley's surprise, Egbert did not promptly launch into a defense of poetry, or a sermon on the joys of reading or the importance of literature. He had other things on his mind. After all, Egbert's memories of Ocean's End were hardly joyous, even from before he was Shunned. And the fact that breeding season was in full swing made his timing especially bad. Males were jealously guarding their harems and were in no mood for intruders.

They hadn't traveled far before they came upon the clan they had heard beneath the ice. Lockley was horrified by what he saw. It was as if they had stumbled onto a battlefield. Pairs of walrus bulls were fighting each other, their huge bodies colliding with sudden violence, their tusks clashing like swords.

"Don't worry," said Egbert, seeing Lockley shudder. "They're just play-fighting. Practicing their skills. The best warriors get the best cows at the beginning of the mating season. If they were fighting for real, they would fight to the death—or surrender."

Lockley was still horrified. "It's so brutal! You're the only walrus I know. . . ."

"As I said, I was a Scholars' apprentice. The Scholars consider themselves above warring and breeding. But this is just life in a walrus clan, Lockley. It's not all that different from most species."

Lockley couldn't imagine anyone less willing to battle to the death than Egbert, unless it was in a war of words. Looking out at the clan, he was also struck by something else: "I can't believe there are walruses bigger than you."

"I told you I wasn't fat for a walrus. Now let's get this over with."

Egbert lurched across the ice in the direction of his old clan, Lockley trailing behind. As soon as they spotted him, a group of bulls moved aggressively to cut Egbert off.

"Stop where you are!" commanded one. "The cows here are spoken for."

A more mature bull came toward them. "Yes, *Egbert*," he said, clearly displeased by Egbert's reappearance.

One of the younger bulls said, "This is Egbert?" and began to laugh. "What's wrong? Couldn't find a seal to mate with?"

The laughter spread, and Lockley stepped forward to defend his friend.

"See here," he said. "That's no way to talk to one of your own. Besides, Egbert is *not* here to find a mate."

"Who's talking?" said one of the bulls, and they all looked around until they noticed, apparently for the first time, that Egbert wasn't alone.

"For the love of fish—he's mated with a penguin!" said one.

Lockley didn't know which made him more angry—the fact that even a group of walruses thought he was a penguin, or that they thought he might actually be Egbert's mate. He was so flummoxed he failed to correct either mistake.

"I am not here to find a mate, nor am I returning to the clan," said Egbert. "I need to speak to the Scholars."

"The Scholars?" said the mature bull. "Have you forgotten you were Shunned?"

"The Shunning!" whispered another, which multiplied into dramatic murmuring.

Egbert turned to Lockley and said, "Let's be on our

way." But when they tried to leave, another pair of young bulls came and blocked them. Both proudly bore many scars earned in battle. They looked Egbert over with contempt. "How does a walrus have such a smooth hide?" said one.

"Yes," said the other, slithering around Egbert and rubbing his side with a fin. "Do the laws of nature not apply where you live? Or are you just afraid to fight?"

"Actually," said Lockley, stepping into view again, "on Neversink we settle disputes in a civilized way, through the mediation of a law-speaker. Unless of course it's something that affects both Tytonia *and* Neversink, in which case the Parliament of Owls is involved. You see, we are an *independent* colony, but still technically a colony of Tytonia in territory-wide affairs."

Usually it was Egbert rendering the auks speechless as he explained the ways of the world. This time Lockley had managed to silence the entire walrus clan, who just looked at him, puzzled.

"It's not as complicated as it sounds," Lockley added, tapping his wings together.

"Never-*what*?" said one of the bulls who had challenged Egbert.

"Sink," said Lockley.

The other bull spoke up: "Are you going to fight or not, Egbert?"

Egbert's body language told the story, and like schoolyard bullies, the young males seemed eager to pick a fight they knew they couldn't lose. But an older cow came forward and took pity on him. "Just let him go," she said. "I'm sure the Scholars would like a chance to humiliate him themselves."

Reluctantly the bulls parted, ushering Egbert toward the wastelands, jeering as he left.

16

LUCY'S LAST STAND

Summer is normally a glorious time for the birds of Neversink. A time of fellowship on Auk's Landing, a time to nest and breed in the everlasting light of those endless days, before the perpetual dark of winter sets in and they spend most of their time at sea, chasing scarcer food supplies and training their young to swim and fish. A bird like Algard Guillemot might never admit it, but Egbert and Ruby had become a part of this fellowship.

Rozbell had turned the auks' seasons upside down. He had exploited fears of a plague on his own island to seize control of Parliament and poach the auks' food supply. His greediness had then led indirectly to the disappearance of their food supply entirely. And now his fiendish new plan to feed himself with the auks' eggs threatened to jeopardize the colony's future by wiping out an entire breeding season. A new kind of darkness had set in—a premature winter. So perhaps you will understand why, despite the sun shining coldly above them, many auks began to say, "The stars are shining on Neversink."

The king followed up his announcement by sending Edmund and his crew of burrowing owls to Neversink to invade the auks' dug-out nests and seize their eggs. The wails of guillemot, murre, razorbill, and puffin families filled the air. A squadron of white pelicans came daily to collect the eggs, their enormous, slow-beating, black-tipped wings becoming objects of foreboding against the concrete sky.

What Rozbell didn't count on was the fact that you can, believe it or not, push a puffin too far. At least, you can push a new mother and abandoned wife too far.

"You want to do what?" said an astonished Algard, when Lucy came to his door.

"I want to kick the burrowing owls out of our burrows! Most of us are bigger than they are, or at least on even terms. And there are way more of us. We don't have to stand for this!"

"I see insanity runs in Lockley's family," said Algard.

"Algard, you know the old saying. Act like a doormat,

expect to end up in front of a door." (This made more sense back then.)

"You're forgetting something," said Algard. "The burrowing owls are just hired beaks. We stand up to them, Rozbell just sends over more owls. Bigger owls. Owls we *won't* be able to stand up to."

"What difference does that make?" Lucy shot back. "If we just roll over and let him take our eggs, we may as well all be dead anyway."

Algard looked at her, wondering where this streak of defiance came from. And why his family had chosen to nest next to the one pair of puffins with some backbone.

"Lucy, I—that is to say—I'll think about it. Okay? In the meantime, just try and make the best of it." Which could have been yet another auk motto.

Algard wasn't the only one to watch Lucy storm off (for she did in fact storm off, as best a puffin can storm, anyway). Astra took note as well. She wondered if there were any owls on Tytonia willing to defy Rozbell half as much.

In the desolate mists of Slog's Hollow, Rozbell was in his owlery, enjoying the trappings of royalty. He wasn't so much perched as he was sprawled among the branches. House sparrows were polishing his new crown while Alf buffed his talons. Rozbell had hoarded the last of the smidgens for himself. From looks of the auk eggs piled up in his owlery, Alf wondered if he was planning to share those, either.

"Your Majesty," said Alf cautiously, "as superb a plan as it was to steal the auks' eggs, their couples produce but one egg each for the breeding system. Even the entire supply would feed us all only temporarily."

Rozbell stood up and shooed away the house sparrows. "Feed us all? Don't be ridiculous. The eggs are for me. I need sustenance to lead us out of this crisis."

"Your Majesty," stammered the elderly owl, still crouched at Rozbell's feet. "If I may . . . others have reported that the number of unexplained deaths seem to be fewer that expected . . . compared to the last time, that is. Some are talking of hunting again—with your permission, of course. Perhaps the Sickness did not return as feared?"

Rozbell kicked him to the ground almost before he could finish speaking. "You're questioning my judgment? The Great Gray Owl wanted to sit there and let everyone perish. I work to save us all, and this is what's being said? This is the gratitude?"

"No . . ."

"So it's just you then?"

The old owl threw himself facedown at Rozbell's feet. He was searching for anything to say that could save himself when a long-eared owl from the Great Northern Forest arrived, holding something in his mouth.

"Just put me down here, good sir," said the mole. The owl complied.

"Well, if it isn't Mr. Mole," said Rozbell. "Do you have any intelligence for me?"

The mole looked around, tapping his forepaws. "You mean, he's not here?"

Rozbell looked around. "Who? Who?"

"The puffin. I led him and his hummingbird friend to the moors, where the puffin fell into a bog. I reported this fact to the wood owls."

Both the mole and Rozbell looked at the long-eared owl for an explanation. "I beg your pardon, Your Majesty," said the owl. "There was a mix-up. There were reports of any number of exotic birds—harlequin ducks, toucans, macaws, parrots, penguins, common loons. . . ."

Rozbell's eyelids began to twitch. "I thought owls were smart!" he screeched. "In the name of the gods, doesn't anyone here know what a puffin is? I mean, they live right over there!

"*You* knew it was the puffin," said Rozbell, turning on the mole. "Why didn't you come to me directly?"

The mole was quavering. "It would have taken quite some time to tunnel back from the moors. I thought telling an owl would be the quickest way to dispatch the puffin." He nodded his head in the direction of the long-eared owl, as if to say, *Blame him*. "I think you'll agree,

I did my part," said the mole.

Rozbell just stared at him. "Yes, you did your part. And now it's done." And with that he jumped down, plucked up the terrified mole, and swallowed him whole. It did not escape the others' notice that Rozbell seemed unconcerned that the mole might be contaminated.

As Rozbell let out a small belch, Feathertop swooped into the owlery, clutching black feathers in his mouth. Right behind him, a large raven glided in on swept-back wings.

"What are those?" said Rozbell. "And who are you?"

"Your Majesty," croaked the raven, his voice hollow and metallic, "I am Klink. I lead a conspiracy of ravens in the north. And those are puffin feathers."

"The escaped puffin?" said Rozbell, looking to Feathertop. "You caught him?"

As Feathertop had a mouthful of feathers, Klink spoke for him. "The eagle did catch him. With a bit of assistance from us, if I may humbly say so."

Klink and Feathertop exchanged a wordless glance. Ravens, being scavengers, were forever trying to curry favor with birds of prey, who would leave juicy food remains for them. When Feathertop failed to capture Lockley, Klink was only too happy to show him the feathers from Lockley's decoy and suggest a plan for convincing Rozbell the puffin was dead.

Rozbell motioned for one of the house sparrows to bring

him the feathers. "Where's the rest of him?" he said, flicking his tail in agitation. "I wanted to see the body myself. I wanted to punt it around like a vole, take it into the woods and let owlets poke it with sticks, and then drop it in the middle of the colonists to let those *fish-eaters* and that *toothwalker* see what happens when you defy authority."

Klink waited for Feathertop to explain, but thinking on his feet was not the eagle's strong suit.

"I apologize, Your Majesty," Klink croaked. "I'm afraid I let my ravens scavenge a bit, to reward them."

"But poking it with sticks!" said Rozbell.

"That would have been delightful, Your Majesty. Still, as far as showing the auks what can happen if they defy authority, may I make a suggestion? Permit me to take the feathers publicly to the dead puffin's wife. I assure you it will have the same effect."

Rozbell, still holding the feathers, fluttered up to a branch near Klink. A wicked grin broke across his face, and he handed the feathers back to the raven. "I've always said you could trust a raven!" he chirped. He then hopped over to a branch near Feathertop. "I didn't bring you all the way here to get help from the *locals*. What have *you* done for me lately? You're supposed to help me hunt, and I'm the one coming up with all the ways to keep us fed. And your appetite is ten times as big!"

Feathertop was stunned by his master's sudden rebuke.

He glanced around the owlery, all too aware that he was being taken down a branch in public. The other birds pretended not to notice.

And so Rozbell sent the raven Klink to Lucy's burrow, further enhancing that bird's reputation as a foreteller of doom. The blackish bird coasted the length of Auk's Landing, a grim sight for all to see, including Lucy, who had stepped outside for a breath of air.

Algard and other nearby auks looked on with pity as the raven dropped to the ground and handed her Lockley's feathers. In true puffin fashion, Lucy bore her grief inwardly, refusing to make a spectacle of her loss before quietly slipping back inside.

Algard had promised Lucy he would think about her plan to rebuff the burrowing owls. And he did. He thought about how foolish it would be to do such a thing. Suicidal, even. And he thought about how nice it would be to live on the other end of Auk's Landing, far away from the troublesome puffins.

But then he was outside when he saw one of the burrowing owls finally come to Lucy's door, despite all the efforts of Egbert to hide her egg by girth or games. And he saw with his own eyes Lucy answer the door holding one of her smidgen pans, he saw her raise the pan above her head, and he saw her bring the pan down with deliberate force on the stunned owl's head, crushing the small hat that sat upon it. He saw the owl stumble away from her door, his eyes glazed over, until he fell backward over a rock, no doubt adding a bump on the back of his head to go with the one on the top. And finally, he saw the owl stand back up on his tall legs, which were shaking either from wooziness or fear, and wobble away from Lucy Puffin's burrow.

Algard, his eyes still wide with disbelief, walked slowly back to his own burrow, alarming his wife with his far-off stare. "What's wrong, Algard?" she asked.

"She brained him," said Algard, half to himself. "Wham," he added, miming the movement with his own wings.

"What are you holding?" his wife asked, and Algard looked into his empty wings.

"Nothing." He had come back from the sea that morning with a completely empty bill. The waters now, for all practical purposes, were dry. *What am I afraid of losing at this point?* thought Algard.

The next morning, sitting on her perch above the colony, Astra was struck by the spectacle of small, stilt-legged burrowing owls being bounced from doorsteps by larger murres, guillemots, and razorbills. Even the less physically imposing puffins found the courage to look the little owls in their amber eyes and clack their bills until the burrowing owls backed off. Astra knew she shouldn't be enjoying this, but the sight of Edmund running back and forth, trying to figure out who to scream at—his cowardly crew or the defiant auks—made her laugh quietly.

"Make them comply!" cried Edmund, who had finally given up trying to solve the problem himself. "It's your *job*."

"Suddenly you respect my authority," said Astra coldly.

Edmund seethed. "Tell Rozbell, or I will!"

Astra spun her head toward the aggrieved owl. "Don't tell me my duties," she said sharply. "For now, stay out of the auks' burrows."

Edmund's crew didn't mind being given an excuse to avoid getting hit, spat at, or generally injured all over again. But Edmund didn't trust Astra. He had always been unnerved by the cool disposition of snowy owls—remote both in personality and in their habitats, preferring much colder climates than most owls. He thought Rozbell should know what was going on, and he wasn't sure Astra would tell him. So when the next squadron of pelicans came, to collect what few eggs the burrowing owls had captured before the revolt, Edmund sent word of what happened.

Rozbell nearly exploded in a vapor of rage. "Stupid, miserable, fish-eating, duck-walking, clown-faced, orange-legged, dough-bellied, flat-footed, funny-flying, ridiculous, silly, pretentious birds!" he screeched, kicking his servant owl in the shins and sending the house sparrows fluttering away like moths. "For the love of fish, why did the gods invent the puffin! *Gewh, gewh, gewh!*"

Rozbell was once again seized by a fit of spastic blinking, as his rage must have sucked the moisture right out of his eyes. Every creature present thought this might be the meltdown so many of them had been waiting for. Finally, Rozbell's blinking subsided and he seemed to calm himself without any outward displays of violence. He remained quiet for several minutes before turning to Feathertop. "Perhaps a personal visit to this . . . *puffin*"—almost choking on the word—"will serve to remind her who her king is."

Feathertop let Rozbell climb aboard, and the pair flew to Neversink, stopping first to speak with Astra, sitting stoically as usual, staring seaward. "Did you not see this happening?" said Rozbell, struggling to keep his composure. "Why didn't you do something?"

"I thought the burrowing owls were just trying to shirk their duties," said Astra.

Rozbell wasn't satisfied by this explanation, but he had more important business. "Show me to this agitator's burrow."

Astra held her ground for a few seconds before pointing in Lucy's direction. "Follow me."

So it was that, as the day dimmed on Neversink, Lucy Puffin's doorstep was darkened by two shadows—one very long, and the other very short. As Lucy went to the door to face Rozbell and Feathertop, Astra perched herself on a rock behind them, watching intently.

"Aren't you going to invite us in?" said Rozbell as he walked right past Lucy into her burrow. Feathertop, though, nearly had to double over just to fit his head in the doorway. Noticing this, Rozbell snapped, "I guess you'll have to wait there."

Of course, Rozbell didn't know for sure that Lucy had an egg of her own. He had come to confront her about the owl she hit over the head, and her unfortunate decision to rally the auks against the home invasions. But Lucy could see the gears of his mind working as he prowled around the living room, seeming to take an interest in everything.

"On the way here," said Rozbell, "I wondered why you, of all the colonists, would take such drastic measures to keep burrowing owls out of your home. The whole point of letting you know your husband was dead was to remind you that no good comes from making trouble. And with your mate dead, what, really, do you have to live for? But rather than going back to minding your own business, you cause even *more* trouble—assaulting one of my soldiers . . . inspiring the others to do the same."

The mention of Lockley was like an icicle in her heart, but as soon as it registered, Lucy felt a wave of nausea hit her. Rozbell walked slowly out of her living room, toward the bedroom. She fled after him, and got there in time to see Rozbell staring at her egg, his face a horrifying, twisted mask of sinister glee. She stood by, paralyzed, as Rozbell rolled the egg from her bedroom toward the front door. He nodded to Feathertop, who extended one of his huge wings and captured the egg, rolling it to the threshold. Lucy regained her senses and ran forward, but with his other wing the eagle batted her against the wall. He rolled the egg all the way outside the burrow, where he clutched it with one of his talons, the razor-sharp tips dimpling the egg's leathery surface.

Lucy felt her breath catch in her throat. Before she could cry out, a small dark object bolted past her, past Feathertop and Rozbell.

"What was that?" said Rozbell. Lucy could only gasp, and when Rozbell looked at Feathertop, he merely shrugged. He was more interested in crushing the egg. "I was going to kill you, or at least torture you," said Rozbell, "but I see now that this will be far more painful."

Lucy's breathing came in spurts as she watched Feathertop carelessly clasping her dear egg. Lockley wouldn't want her to give in, but he wouldn't want this, either. She was about to beg Rozbell for mercy when the unthinkable happened.

Behind Rozbell and Feathertop, a chorus of hoarse *arrr*s and shrill, hissing *peeeee*s swelled like some immense, out-of-tune symphony. A startled Feathertop released the egg, which began to roll down the grassy slope. While he and Rozbell turned to see what was causing the ruckus, Lucy slipped by them and grabbed the egg before it could roll down against the rocks.

Once she had saved her egg, Lucy turned her attention to all the noise, and she was as shocked as Feathertop and Rozbell to discover that they were surrounded by an army of auks, stamping their feet, snapping their bills, and protesting at the top of their lungs. And at the head of the black-and-white force was Algard Guillemot, and hovering next to him was Ruby, a blur of angry energy.

Algard stepped forward to speak. "Unless you are here to offer your condolences for Lockley's death," he said, "you have no business with Lucy Puffin."

"That goes double for you, Featherbrain!" said Ruby, and the sound of her tiny voice filled Lucy with joy.

Rozbell's eyes nearly popped out of his head. Then the spastic blinking started again. The pygmy owl tried to turn his head away, but there were auks everywhere he looked. Humiliated and angry, Rozbell wanted to order Feathertop to attack. Let the fearsome eagle take out two or three, the rest would scatter like cowards. But his blinking—his physical defect on display for all to see—plus the recent evidence with the burrowing owls that the auks might actually stand up for themselves . . . all this planted a seed of doubt in Rozbell's mind. His insecurity got the better of him.

With Feathertop waiting for his orders, and Algard waiting for a reaction, Rozbell half turned to Lucy, partially hiding his face, and said, "If you think this is over, you're dreadfully mistaken." He and Feathertop then flew off, leaving the colony to wonder what would come next.

"Ruby . . . oh, Ruby!" said Lucy. "And Algard, thank you! All of you!" Most of the auks merely grunted and shuffled off.

"You showed a great amount of courage, standing up to the owls," said Algard, "and we are sorry for your loss."

He left Lucy alone with Ruby, who perched right on top of her bill, forcing her to cross her eyes to see the hummingbird.

"Lucy, what are *condolences*? What loss was Algard talking about?"

Lucy took Ruby back inside and showed her Lockley's feathers. She told her about the raven's visit, and then explained that Egbert was gone, too. "You're all I have left, little one."

"Lucy, Lockley's not dead!" said Ruby. Just to be sure, she took a closer look at the feathers, and darted her tongue out at a white splotch of goo. "Marsh-mallow! These are from the decoy!"

"Decoy?"

"Sure! Let's see, there was the escape, then the tunnels,

the badger, the mole who was a mole, the moors, the Teeth of the Moors, the decoy, the highlands, the eagle, and then the *second* escape!"

"Ruby, slow down!" said Lucy, but in truth, her heart was beating like the hummingbird's wings. "Tell me what happened?"

"I just did," said Ruby. "Do you want the long version?"

Lucy smiled. "Come in, I'll boil you some sugar water, and you can tell me everything." Which Ruby did, up to the point where Feathertop chased Lockley off Murre Mountain.

"And I know Featherbrain didn't catch him," said Ruby, "because if he had, he wouldn't have had to use those decoy feathers to prove Lockley was dead. He's just trying to cover his tail feathers with Rozbell!" But when Ruby tried to explain why Lockley hadn't come straight back, why he felt he had to venture to Ocean's End first, Lucy became worried again.

"He's still in danger," she said quietly as Ruby inhaled more sugar water. Then she remembered there was something she'd forgotten to tell Ruby. She led the hummingbird to the bedroom and showed her the new egg.

"Wow, it's bigger than me!" said Ruby, alighting on top of it.

Lucy also told Ruby the horrible news about Rozbell's plan to take their eggs. "Egbert was helping me hide it before they sent him away," she said, her voice rigid with anger. "Ruby, we have to think of something to do until Lockley returns. Or . . . in case he doesn't."

"We'll figure something out," Ruby assured her. "And if we have time, maybe we can even figure out a way to get Egbert back?" she asked, trying to sound as if she didn't care one way or the other.

Lucy took her to the kitchen and fed her sugar water until Ruby couldn't drink any more. Yes, they had to think of something. The solidarity the colony had just showed would not last for long. They were all on the verge of starving. And she knew Rozbell would be back, if not for their eggs, then for something even worse. This was far from over.

IN THE TEMPLE OF KNOWLEDGE

Lockley had never been so cold in his life. Egbert, on the other hand, burned with shame as they crossed the barren ice. Lockley was thoroughly disoriented by the featureless landscape. In all directions, the land spread out like frosted glass, apparently deserted. But appearances are deceiving in the Arctic.

The Arctic may appear to be a white wasteland, but Egbert knew very well there was more to fear than the sting of the cold and the bite of the wind. Food was always a problem. The "land" around the North Pole was just frozen ice. Unless they were at the water's edge, seals and walruses had to carve holes in the ice in order to fish. Going in was no problem. But sometimes, waiting for them when they came out was the beast feared by all—the bear known by his prey as the White Death. And if the bear became impatient, he had no qualms about tracking down a walrus clan or a seal pod.

Lockley was aware of these dangers, too, for Egbert had told him, numerous times, when telling him tales of his ancestral home. His primary concern, though, was freezing to death. He fluffed up his underfeathers against the cold and told himself that if he kept moving, he might at least warm up some.

"Egbert, why are the Scholars so far from the clan? Do you even know where we're going?"

"They aren't part of my clan," said Egbert. "Or any clan. They are remote both in body and spirit. By distancing themselves from the base needs of warring and mating, they can concentrate on the higher arts of learning."

"They don't mate?" said Lockley. "Do they live forever?"

"I'm sure they've studied the possibility," said Egbert, his enormous body spraying cold, crystalline chips in Lockley's face as he slid across the ice. "But no, they are replaced by candidates, chosen by the Scholars themselves."

"And you were a candidate?"

"I was," said Egbert, his voice heavy and wistful. "Even the clan kings have no authority over the Scholars. They sit above all."

Well that explains a lot, thought Lockley. He could easily imagine how well Egbert would have fit in, lording his intellect over his more brutish kin. *No wonder he was forever being surprised by the auks' capacity to ignore him!* Lockley's wandering thoughts at least had the benefit of taking his mind off the cold. But he was completely caught off guard when Egbert finally said, "We're here."

Lockley looked up. Nothing Egbert had ever told him about the library prepared him for what he saw. In what should have been the middle of nowhere was a strange, almost surreal temple of ice, where learning itself assumed the form of architecture. Great slabs of ice were carved by tusk with the writings of the Scholars and their pupils. They formed a pathway into a large courtyard with more carved ice sheets serving as both wall and sculpture, and still others formed more pathways that led off to other ice chambers. Sunlight refracting through the colossal ice texts made them sparkle like engraved crystal, and both Egbert and Lockley stood awed by the prisms of light—the radiance of accumulated wisdom.

Emotions flooded Egbert as he wandered through the library of the Scholars for the first time since his Shunning. He made his way through the courtyard to what he remembered was the main reading room, and again he had to catch his breath. Shimmering amid the ice was an exquisite ivory building, made from walrus tusk. Two enormous

doors, leather hides stretched over a frame of bones, stood open to a dark entryway. On the inside of each door was mounted a long, saber-like walrus tusk, the pair of which could be folded into an ivory X to lock the doors. Egbert peered into the darkness and said, "In here."

Lockley followed Egbert into the cavernous entryway, which led to an even larger central room hung with tapestries made of hide. Light filtered through a translucent roof of ice to an ivory table the length of a whale, it seemed to Lockley. And sitting around the table were nine of the largest walruses Lockley had ever seen, each poring over ice texts, seemingly lost in thought and oblivious to their visitors.

Egbert stood there, watching them work. Some were reading, others writing, using ivory tusks to carve lines and symbols into sheets of pure ice, frosted white from cold. The writers would occasionally stop to brush away the frozen residue that built up along the narrow grooves like salt crystals. One by one the Scholars noticed Egbert. And Lockley.

"Well, well, well," said one. "Egbert, have you moved to the South Pole?"

Lockley, who had been frozen with awe, suddenly thawed with irritation. "For the *love . . . of . . . fish*! Even the most educated animals on the planet confuse me with a penguin? I'm a *puffin*, for crying out loud! We live just off the edge of the Arctic. If you ever bothered to leave your blooming library once in a while, you might have met one of us!"

The Scholars just stared at this strange eruption of both color and emotion. Even Egbert was shocked by Lockley's outburst. "If all puffins are as volatile as you," said one, "then I'm glad I haven't met one before now." The others nodded vigorously in agreement.

A different Scholar spoke up. "I'm sure I am not alone among my learned friends in wondering what you are doing here, Egbert. With a puffin."

"My learned friend makes an excellent point," said a third. "I believe you were Shunned." The Scholars mumbled reverently at the mere mention of the word.

Egbert bowed his head, either out of reverence or humiliation; Lockley was unsure which. He had never seen Egbert struggle so to speak.

"I assure you I would not have presumed to return unless it was a matter of great urgency," said Egbert. "Lives are at stake."

"Ours?" said a Scholar.

"No, the lives of all the innocent creatures of Neversink," said Lockley, stepping forward. When they heard this, the Scholars immediately lost interest.

"Such concerns are quite literally beneath us," one Scholar explained. When Lockley began to protest, Egbert motioned for him to be quiet, and moved forward.

"Naturally you shouldn't concern yourselves with the plight of an insignificant bird sanctuary far south of here," said Egbert. "Which is why we would never ask for your help in researching the knowledge we need. We simply beg the privilege of access to the library for ourselves. Only for today."

"We don't give out *guest passes*."

"My learned friend is quite right. This is a place of scholarship, for those who have *devoted their lives* to scholarship."

"Oh, but I have!" said Egbert. "I know you considered it heresy at the time, but perhaps now that I've made some headway . . ." He proceeded to explain to them his invention of the book, with all its benefits and improvements. "Imagine," he added, "texts that can survive the melting that occurs every ten thousand years or so . . . vast amounts of wisdom and entertainment have been lost!"

"Enough!" said a Scholar, slamming his fin into the table. "This *book* . . . it lacks the beauty of the ice texts. And their humility."

"My learned friend is quite right. Trying to make your work outlast an ice age is the height of arrogance. Besides, the materials and labor you describe to produce one of these . . . *books* . . . quite impractical for Ocean's End."

"But Ocean's End doesn't have to be the only place

of learning!" said Egbert.

A collective gasp echoed through the ivory chamber. "We've been through this before," said another. "Our vagabond pupil here would have us teaching the snails to read and write."

"They could slime their words across the page."

The Scholars let out a great collective laugh—the kind of haughty, sneering laugh that only the most overeducated animals are capable of. Egbert could see what he was up against.

"Forgive our rudeness," said one, addressing Lockley. "We should have properly introduced ourselves. We are the heads of the Nine Departments of Wisdom."

On cue, the Scholars of Philosophy, Religion, Law, Marine Biology, Ancient History, Ancient Literature, Less-Ancient Literature, Literature of the Middle Ages, and Contemporary Literature each bowed in turn as their names were pronounced.

"If you have Scholars of ancient literature *and* literature of the Middle Ages, why do you need a Scholar of less-ancient literature?" asked Lockley.

The Scholar of Less-Ancient Literature let out a shriek.

"Nine is a perfect number," said one. "It allows us to have a tiebreaking vote at faculty meetings."

"But you've never discussed adding a new area of scholarship over the years?"

"What department of wisdom have we failed to account for?"

"*Non*marine biology?" said Lockley.

"Too dull."

"World culture?"

"Too broad."

"Gender politics in northern epic poetry?"

"Too specialized."

"Really, Mr. Puffin," said another Scholar, "this is bordering on impudence."

The others agreed. Egbert, meanwhile, had used the diversion to think of a new line of persuasion: "You see how ignorant my lowly puffin friend is," he said.

"Hey!" said Lockley, but his protest was drowned out by sighs of agreement from the Scholars.

"Think of how impressed—awestruck—he would be," Egbert continued, "if he were allowed to gaze upon the wonderment of your achievements. I dare say he will be recounting this glorious moment among his own kind for the rest of his miserable, unwalruslike days!"

This gave the Scholars pause. The idea of having their greatness talked about beyond Ocean's End, even by *lesser* creatures, seemed to appeal to them. One pulled another aside and whispered something to him, and he in turn passed the message to another, and so on down the line. The last Scholar nodded, then spoke.

"An interesting point, Egbert. However, you were Shunned, and we have no policy in place for Unshunning you, even temporarily."

"Couldn't you vote on one now?" Lockley wondered.

"That would take years of contemplation," said the Scholar. "Therefore, your request is denied. We ask that you leave the library as soon as possible."

Ushered rudely outside, Lockley and Egbert had the doors shut in their faces and heard the tusk-handles on the other side clack together as the doors were locked. Lockley thought he'd never met a more unreasonable group of creatures in his life. "What do we do now, Egbert?"

Egbert slowly shook his head. "We leave."

"That's it?" He was appalled that Egbert would give up so easily after coming so far.

"That's it. We have to go."

Still in disbelief that their trip had come to nothing, Lockley took one last look at the towering temple of ice and followed Egbert back toward the empty exile of the Arctic.

"What do I do now, Lockley? I've been banned from the only two places I've ever called home."

Lockley had never seen Egbert so deflated. He gave his rough hide a gentle pat. "I know how you feel, old boy. I may not have a home to go home to either."

"I'm sorry," said Egbert. "I'm thinking only of myself,

as usual. That was the whole point of this journey—to help you."

"Psst."

"Did you say something?"

"Not me," said Lockley. "Maybe it was the wind." Indeed, it seemed to howl all about them, filling up the vast empty spaces. But then Lockley heard it again. "Egbert, I think the wind just called your name."

"Over here."

They both turned and saw what appeared to be a walrus peeking his head out from behind the library. He motioned to them. When they got nearer, Lockley saw that it was Barold, the Scholar of Less-Ancient Literature. He wondered if the Scholar was still nursing a grudge for the way Lockley had insulted him.

"There's a structure behind the main library," Barold said to Egbert, "built since you left. The Scholars needed more space. They decided anything not deemed *pure* walrus literature would be restricted to this building. I'm guessing whatever you need that pertains to your friend's home would be in there."

"And you can let us in?" said Egbert. "Won't we be seen?"

"The other Scholars rarely go there, concentrating as they do on the *pure* literature. I doubt anyone will take much note of a couple of walruses shuffling about there."

"Why are you doing this?" said Lockley. "Couldn't you be Shunned, too?"

To answer, Barold looked squarely at Egbert. "I may not agree with all our former candidate's ideas. But I do think the Scholars should be looking outward, not inward. Here is a clear case where knowledge might do some practical good, and we don't want to share it."

It was Lockley's turn to look at Egbert. "I'm sure the Great Auk would say that sharing doesn't do much good if the pupils aren't listening."

"If you're referring to my lack of success on Neversink," said Egbert, "no one is to blame but me. I just assume that what's important to me should be important to everyone."

"All right, all right," said Barold. "We can all beat ourselves up later. Right now we need to get to those shelves."

The three quietly made their way to a structure Egbert had never seen before. It was far less magnificent than the main library, built of raw tusk and hide. Inside, it was barren but for a single long study table, made of ice, and shelves stacked floor to ceiling with ice sheets.

Barold and Egbert moved from shelf to shelf, running their fins along the spines of ice, which were organized according to a cataloging system that remained a mystery to Lockley. Finally Egbert stopped and pulled forth one of the great frozen tablets, laying it carefully on the table. "Here it is," he said solemnly. "'The Tricking of Sedna.'"

The title was completely unreadable to Lockley, of course. But he was surprised to find himself admiring the rhythmic beauty of the angled marks and abstract symbols, tracing the etched grooves with his wing tips, wondering if there *was* something to the written word.

"How did the walruses come up with this?" he wondered aloud.

Egbert looked at Barold, who stretched himself out along the floor and rolled onto his side, so that his massive hide was like a scroll of gray parchment, and his hide scars like ancient runes or cave drawings. Lockley thought back to the hide tapestries in the main reading room and realized they were not decorated—they were actual hides of past walruses, scarred with history.

"Our hides have long told stories about us," Barold explained. "The wars we've fought, the battles for our mates . . . even the kings we served, for in olden days our king would brand all the males in his clan."

"These are amazing!" said Lockley, admiring the ice texts. A proud Egbert pulled forth sagas of long-gone walrus kings and warriors with names like Tusker, Brymley, and Harald. Sagas of heroes and villains, intruders and outlaws. Then Lockley remembered he was admiring the work of those haughty walruses from the library, which lessened his enthusiasm.

Egbert also seemed to shrink a bit when he remembered

the purpose of this new reading room. "There will probably be a story about me in here someday," he said ruefully. "Shelved among the notorious and the Shunned."

Barold reminded them what they were there for, and Egbert turned back to the story of Sedna. "Egbert, old boy," said Lockley, "if this works, I'll take back every bad thing I ever said about book learning."

Egbert just snorted and began scanning the text silently while Lockley grew impatient. But Egbert ignored him until he had finished reading the familiar tale, most of which he had heard from the Great Auk. The written version had the same ending as the Great Auk's, with Sedna becoming a vengeful goddess. Egbert had been hoping the scholarly text would include additional notes. As Lockley looked on anxiously, Egbert's whiskers began to twitch. "Ah, here it is—the spirit journey!"

"What does it say? What does it say?"

"'One must journey to the bottom of the sea, to Sedna's lair. She is heavily guarded, and there are many obstacles. If one survives the trip and is granted an audience, allow her to request a favor, in hopes that she will forgive you.'"

"How does she decide whether to grant you an audience?"

Egbert skimmed the text again. "It's not specific," he said. "It just says, 'If one is deemed worthy of the spirit journey.'"

Lockley seemed discouraged by this. "Egbert, you've seen what happens when I try to play the hero. Besides, how am I supposed to dive all the way to the bottom of the sea? How would any bird do that?"

"Uh-oh," said Egbert, reading more.

"It gets worse?"

"We need biteweed," said Egbert. "It's a plant. You must eat it before undertaking the journey."

"Why is that bad?"

"Because although my knowledge of botany is limited, I'm quite sure biteweed is exceedingly rare. At the very least, I'm certain it doesn't grow at Ocean's End." He looked at Barold, who shook his head.

Lockley was ashamed of how relieved he felt hearing this. *The Great Auk would certainly be proud of me*, he thought, absently fingering his clamshell necklace. And then, it hit him. "Egbert!" he said, digging into his breast feathers to grab the clamshell and hold it up for the walruses to see.

"I'm not hungry," said Egbert.

"I could have one clam," said Barold, reaching for it.

"No!" said Lockley. "The Great Auk gave me this and said, '*Open it when you need to.*'"

He pulled open the clamshell, and inside was a sprig of thorny green plant. He showed it to Egbert, who gently poked it with his fin. "Ouch!"

"Egbert, do you think . . . have you ever seen biteweed before?"

"No," said Egbert, "but those thorns would certainly bite back if you tried to eat it. And I can't imagine the Great Auk giving you such a thing without a good reason."

Lockley stared at the sprig a bit longer. "Egbert, I'm afraid."

"Just think of it as spiny sea urchin," said Egbert.

"I don't eat sea urchin!" Lockley retorted. "Besides, that's not what I meant."

Egbert took the stalk of biteweed and snapped it in two. "We're in this together, my dear. We'll find an ice hole, and we'll eat this at the same time and see what happens."

Lockley took his half. "Thank you, Egbert. You are a true friend."

And so they thanked Barold and sneaked out of the library, returning to the void of the endless ice. Egbert looked wistfully over his shoulder as they set out, as if regretting his decision all those years ago to defy the Scholars and deprive himself of this magnificent temple of learning—a place where he really could belong.

Lockley noticed this too, and he felt, even more than the bitter cold, the burden of responsibility for having exposed his proud friend to ridicule and danger—after endangering Ruby's life as well. To say nothing of what Lucy must be going through back on Neversink. How could a goddess think him anywhere close to worthy of a favor?

Before long they reached a pair of openings in the ice. "They look like seal holes," said Egbert. "Might be a tight fit for me."

They wished each other good luck, and then each placed his piece of biteweed in his mouth and carefully chewed and swallowed, grimacing at the spiky texture and bitter taste. Egbert gestured toward the hole. "After you, my dear."

THE ODDEST SEA

It was as if Lockley had pierced a membrane separating one reality from another. He could scarcely see, but he flapped his wings and flew away as fast as he could from the surface, toward the ocean's twilight zone. He came alongside a colossal sperm whale, also diving straight down with deliberate speed.

"Is someone after you, too?" said the whale.

"I beg your pardon?" said Lockley. But the whale didn't bother to answer. He pumped his massive flukes and disappeared into the darkness, leaving Lockley alone. Lockley stopped flying and just bobbed there, suspended in the void like a lonely planet, wondering what on earth was happening to him.

He grabbed a passing flashlight fish and squeezed its tail so that it lit up like a wand. The eerie illumination showed Lockley that he was anything but alone. The surrounding waters teemed with catfish, dogfish, and sea horses—but these versions looked just like their namesakes on land, except with fins in place of legs. Lockley was knocked sideways as a skittering zebra fish swam by, pursued by an enormous sea lion.

Lockley regained his balance, and it occurred to him that Egbert wasn't with him. Or at least, not that he could see. He captured another flashlight fish and gave it a squeeze. He was rewarded with a frightful sight—a pair of bulging eyes. "Ah! Who's there?"

"Hello!" said the silvery fish. "The Salmon of Knowledge here, at your service. One taste of my flesh, and all that is necessary shall be known to you. . . ."

"Yoo-hoo! Over here!"

Lockley turned and saw a red herring beckoning to him.

"Follow me!" said the red herring, and Lockley, without so much as a *good day* to the salmon, took off after the strangely alluring red fish. The herring shot out of sight, over a ridge and into a crevasse, flashing into view on occasion to keep Lockley on his tail.

As soon as Lockley entered the crevasse, he knew he'd made a mistake. From the nooks and crannies of the walls emerged every gruesome form of night hunter: The snapping jaws of a moray eel nipped his heels. A gauntlet of octopus arms barely missed snaring him. Anemones and sea wasps cracked their whiplike stingers at him. Lockley escaped them all and shot out of the crevasse onto a plateau of sea bottom, where he found himself in a forest.

But what was a forest doing buried in the ocean? Lockley wondered, looking at the trees laden with monstrous red fruits. Only they weren't fruits. Upon closer inspection, Lockley saw they were hams. Hams growing on trees.

"The salt water cures them!" said a fish swimming among the dangling hocks.

"But why is there ham growing at the bottom of the sea?" said Lockley.

"For the carnivores, of course," the fish answered.

"Carnivores?" Then Lockley noticed the piles of clean-picked bones littering the ocean bottom. Suddenly, a very toothy tiger shark—a strange beast with the head of a tiger and the body of a shark—ambushed him from behind a tree, closing his fanged mouth inches away from Lockley's throat. The attack sent Lockley tumbling head over heels through the water, and when he righted himself, he flew as fast as he could through the forest without looking back, though he could feel the predator bearing down on him. This should have been the puffin's domain. His little torpedo of a body squirted through the water with ease. But the shark stayed right on his tail.

Lockley flew as hard as he could, dodging the ham hocks, drumsticks, pork chops, beef tenderloins, legs of lamb, and briskets that dangled from the tendon-like branches of the grotesque trees. Barely avoiding a side of beef, he dove through the entrance of a sea cave, hoping against hope that it led somewhere besides an early grave. The tunnel narrowed, and continued to narrow, until Lockley spied his only escape route: a small hole that looked too small for a sparrow, much less a puffin. There was no other choice, though, and so he tucked his wings and hoped for the best.

Lockley felt the sides of the hole rake his body, but he just squeezed through. Moments after he did, there was a muffled *squatch* as the tiger shark swam into the opening and stuck like a cork. The beast's menacing look was replaced by helpless surprise followed rather quickly by extreme rage. Lockley resisted the urge to taunt him and instead turned to swim far away as fast as possible. When he did, he was once again face-to-face with a bulging pair of eyes. "Ah!"

"Hello! Salmon of Knowledge again. Bet you wish you'd paid closer attention the last time."

"Yes, well," stammered Lockley, "be that as it may . . ."

"As I was saying before you so rudely interrupted me—and I suggest you let me finish this time—one taste of my flesh—"

Before he could finish, Lockley swallowed him whole and let out an enormously satisfying belch. "What an insufferable know-it-all he was."

Lockley suddenly began to feel quite ill. It felt like the salmon was trying to swim back up his gullet. He made a mental note never to combine biteweed and talking fish. The ocean began to glow as if the sun were rising from some distant undersea ridge, until the light was so bright Lockley couldn't see at all. His blindness was temporary, however, and when he regained his sight, he could see . . . *everything.*

Lockley was looking up at a tree of indescribable size that seemed to grow from the bottom of the world to the top of the sky. From three colossal roots the tree branched out into the past, the present, and the future. Lockley watched the seasons change as the red bird of fall, the white bird of winter, the blue bird of spring, and the green bird of summer migrated from one part of the tree to another. Thought and Memory flitted among the branches, as did Reason and Knowledge. In the past, an owl, an auk, a raven, and a merlin perched in the tree. In the present, only the owl, the raven, and the merlin remained. And in the future, the apes of the ground were climbing among the branches with the birds. Encircling the full girth of the tree was a serpent, gnawing at the roots, even as a great eagle launched attacks on it, clawing at the serpent's eyes. Lockley was terrified, for he did not understand what he saw.

Gluttony begets suffering, came a voice, unseen but not unkind. *Will you never learn?*

Sand blew up from the sea bottom, clouding the waters. When they cleared again, Lockley saw no tree, but instead a forest of kelp, great fanning stalks swayed by the currents. Lockley entered the forest, and the ocean floor fell away from him, plunging him into the abyss. Lockley felt himself carried down as if by a surging river into a sunless sea.

Come to me.

Lockley was in the presence of an alien form with the body of a seal and the head of a bird. But the bird face was immobile and strangely lifeless. *What happened to the tree?* he tried to say. But his sodden words fell voiceless from his mouth.

The World Tree was, is, and shall be, came the answer, in the voice of a she. *Only your knowledge of it differs.* Her words, from the unmoving mouth, seemed invisible, inaudible. As if she was simply putting thoughts into Lockley's head. She came before him; her shadow devoured him. Lockley could see now that the head was indeed lifeless. It wasn't real—it was a wooden mask. And the body was not the body of a seal, but was covered in sealskins.

What happened next horrified Lockley. Sedna pulled off her mask and skins and showed Lockley her true goddess form. As the mask came off, her bundled-up hair scrolled into the water, impossibly long and black. And tangled in the forever-flowing strands was all the filth and refuse of the sea: bones, teeth, and eyes of half-devoured fish; pieces of skin and scales; decayed plant matter; barnacles, limpets, and other parasites; dismembered starfish arms; and other horrid dead and half-dead things, so that she was transformed into a hideous monster.

Lockley could not hide his disgust, and Sedna, ashamed, pushed back her filthy tresses. Then, like the frightful squid she resembled, she bolted from him into darkness.

"No—I have to save Neversink!" Lockley called after her, but his cries felt mute.

What can I offer that hasn't already been rejected? came the answer from the void.

Lockley made no reply. Instead he closed his mouth and opened his mind and heart, hoping Sedna would see the truth of what had happened, and understand. And he submitted himself to whatever she required of him.

There was a stillness, and then Lockley felt himself in her presence again. Her grotesque, naked face was near his, and she extended one of her long, hairless arms toward his bill. "Such beautiful colors," she said wistfully. "They remind me of my seashell combs. My hair was once the envy of the gods. I can no longer use them." And she held up her two fingerless hands for Lockley to see.

Lockley understood. Cautiously approaching her, he

waded through the black rivers of hair, using his bill to comb out the bones and eyes and half-devoured parts that were knotted in the strands. With sadness he pulled forth whole fish, sand eels and char among them, that he knew must be from Neversink, the waste of his reckless protest. It seemed to take hours, but when he was finally done, Lockley was stunned by the transformation. There was now an alluring beauty to this strange figure as her dark locks extended themselves in the currents like the branches of a sea fan. She then instructed him how to plait the hair into two long braids, so that it would not catch as much of the ocean's filth. Though not as wildly beautiful, the braids made her seem more serene, and—if Lockley had known the term—girlish, like the innocent who had been wooed by the petrel and had vowed never to be tricked again.

Sedna pulled out a large half shell of a giant clam which, to Lockley's wonder, was filled with water that was not the water of the sea. And he saw that when she bent over the dish, an imperfect image of herself appeared in the other water. She looked upon herself and then, neither smiling nor frowning, put the dish away and turned back to Lockley.

"Return to Neversink," she said. "The suffering caused by me shall end." Before sending Lockley away, she cautioned, "The suffering caused by your ruler is beyond my control."

Lockley continued to watch her, transfixed.

"But know this," said the goddess, now swimming gracefully about and occasionally pulling on her new braids. "No false ruler may perch in the World Tree." She smiled, clearly pleased by her generosity.

"Thank you," said Lockley, hiding rather well the fact that he had no idea what she meant him to do with this information. The next thing he knew, a storm blew up from the bottom of the sea, and Lockley was lost in a cloud of dust and freezing water. The darkness closed around him in an icy grip. He began to swim up as fast as he could, fearing that he had angered the goddess and silently wishing that if there was a puffin heaven, it included fish smidgens and cranberry scones. Up and up he went, feeling a lightness under his wings and rising at an incredible rate. And just as the murkiness of the ocean's depths fell away and the waters brightened where the sea touched the sky, Lockley blacked out.

Lockley awoke on the ice, lying near the hole he had dived through. Egbert was there too, sort of. Apparently he had tried to enter his seal-hole tail-first, and he was stuck half in and half out of the water. It looked as if someone had used Egbert to plug a leak. Somehow he had managed to fall asleep in this position.

"Egbert, wake up, old boy."

Lockley finally roused him, and then used his bill to chip away at the hole until Egbert could wriggle free. "Oh dear, Lockley. I don't know what happened."

"I take it you didn't make a spirit journey?"

"Not that I'm aware," said Egbert. "Although I did have the strangest dream. I was walking along a beach with a carpenter, and dozens and dozens of happy oysters followed us, and then we ate them all."

"We don't need Sigmund Freud to analyze that one," said Lockley.

Egbert just looked at him. "You've been spending far too much time with Ruby."

But as Lockley prepared to tell Egbert about his journey, he wondered . . . did he have a dream as well? It had seemed real when it was happening, but it seemed less real now. Egbert was eager to hear about it, though. "Egbert, I'm not sure . . . what if I was just dreaming too?"

Egbert stroked his whiskers thoughtfully, as he was wont to do. "It is called a *spirit journey.* Perhaps it's not meant to seem real?"

Lockley took little comfort in this. The only thing to do was return home and see if things were different. But they were now quite far from the ocean, and after what they had been through, it seemed to take twice as long to slog back across the ice. The wind's claws seemed sharper, too, and Lockley's empty stomach ached. He and Egbert would both need a solid meal to make it back to Neversink.

If you've ever been alone with the wind, you know this elemental force is responsible for more frightful sounds than any other natural phenomenon. Lockley knew this too, but as they skirted a snowbank, something stopped Lockley in his tracks. To their left the snow ran in ripples, as if the incoming sea had frozen in waves. "Egbert, did you hear that?"

Egbert paused, and both stood listening. Almost like a whisper, there was a rustling of snow. The bright white ground began to tremble. Slowly, dozens of pairs of white wings emerged, shaking off their white powder, followed by dozens of long white necks.

"Swans!" said Egbert as Lockley grabbed his fin.

The lamentation of swans exploded from the ground and took to the air, graceful and powerful in flight in a way Lockley knew he could never achieve. He watched with admiration and envy. "I guess we scared them."

"That's rather odd," said Egbert. "I wouldn't think they would be spooked by us. Normally swans would only roust themselves like that because of danger."

"Maybe they were afraid you would sit on them," said Lockley.

"Hardy-har."

The wind picked up again, twisting the curtain of falling snow left in the swans' wake. Lockley froze again.

"Egbert, do you hear that?"

They both stood listening in the snow, staring at the nothing that was there. And then out of nothing it came forth, as if the white storm had suddenly rematerialized in a terrifying framework of white fur and black eyes.

Egbert said calmly, "Fly, Lockley. Fly."

"No! I can't leave you."

But there was no time for a quarrel. The white bear's nose twitched furiously, parsing their scent. He had patches of fur missing and a broken claw. A warrior, thought Lockley, and then he noticed one of the bear's wounds—a long scar over his right shoulder. A tusk wound. This one had been hunting walruses.

The bear unleashed a terrible roar that drowned out even the roar of the wind and the sea. A roar so violent Lockley thought the sound alone would be fatal. Before he or Egbert could react, the bear attacked in a blur of white, and Lockley, knocked back from the sheer force of it, was horrified to see the bear's claws dug into Egbert's sides, his teeth sunk into Egbert's shoulder. Only Egbert's enormous weight kept him from being overwhelmed, and he managed to stab a tusk into the bear's already injured shoulder. The bear howled in pain, and backed away.

Lockley hoped against hope the bear was retreating. Instead he raised himself up on his hind legs, towering over Egbert in a fearsome pose, drawing back a daggered paw to strike. Casting aside all common sense, Lockley ran forward and launched himself at the bear. He heard Egbert cry, "*No!*" just before that massive white paw struck him a blow across the face, sending him sliding across the ice.

The last think Lockley remembered seeing was Egbert looking upon the bear, twisted sideways because of Lockley's brave attack, and throwing himself forward just as the bear turned back to face him. Their collision shook the earth, tooth met claw, the ice cracked, and the white ground blossomed with bright red flowers.

THE RETURN

For the second time, Lockley awoke on the ice, cold, confused, and in pain. Where was he? What was that hill in the distance? He came to his feet, unsteady, and wobbled toward it, and slowly he remembered. There was Egbert, lying motionless in the crater made by his own body. His tusks and his bristly face were stained with blood. Nearby lay the white bear, sprawled on a massive spiderweb of fractured ice.

"Oh, Egbert," said Lockley, his voice soft and sad. "This is all my fault."

A soft *whoosh* of air escaped from the walrus's nostrils, and his eyes rolled open.

"Egbert?"

"Am I . . . alive?"

"Say that again!"

"Say what?" he groaned, barely audible.

"Egbert! Egbert! You're alive! You're alive! You won! You won!"

Egbert let out another moan. "What did I win?"

"The fight! The fight!"

Egbert gave his head a shake. "Something wrong . . . hearing double . . ."

Lockley was embarrassed by his emotional outburst, but he couldn't help himself. To have his friend lying here, alive, against terrible odds! For as anyone knows, a walrus is poorly matched against an adult polar bear. Even a full-grown bull in fighting shape, to say nothing of a flabby male who had given up fighting for scholarship.

But given no choice, Egbert's instincts had shown themselves, and he had met the bear with terrific force. He had thrown the full weight of his body forward and speared him with his tusks. The bear was too big and too strong, though, and would have killed Egbert but for a tactical mistake. The sting of those ivory knives made him flinch. He spun behind Egbert and climbed onto his back. Maybe Egbert knew what he was doing, or maybe it was a fluke reaction in the face of fear. Whatever the truth, just as the bear opened his jaws aimed at Egbert's throat, Egbert tucked his fins and flopped over like a giant mackerel. The earthquake when they hit the ice must have rattled the ice shelves of the Scholars. Egbert knocked himself unconscious, but the bear's back was broken. He died with a pathetic moan.

They both studied the massive cloud of fur next to Egbert. The bear's claws were full of walrus hide, blackened with blood. Egbert was strangely humbled. "It was luck, wasn't it?"

"What makes you say that?" said Lockley. "You fought like a warrior!"

"Even so," and he shook his head. "I could never have taken him one-on-one."

"Well, you certainly didn't have much help from me," said Lockley. "Come on, old boy. There's no reason to be modest for the first time in your life. Your hide's not smooth now."

Egbert smiled, but weakly. Lockley realized he was badly shaken by the battle, and so he left his scarred friend there to rest while he caught fish for them both. When Lockley returned, Egbert seemed to be his old self, bellowing with his customary melodrama, "Oh, Lockley, I am weary unto death!" before devouring the small feast Lockley had set before him. Egbert started to nod off, but Lockley was upon him instantly.

"Egbert, get up. Get up!" He tugged at his friend's whiskers until he came awake. "We've got to get back to Neversink! *Posthaste!*"

"Excellent use of an official-sounding word or phrase," said a groggy Egbert, but Lockley didn't hear him. He was already at the water, wishing dearly to find his home and his family intact.

From her perch far away, Astra watched peacefully as a small puffin hit the shores of Neversink and bumbled to a stop, followed soon thereafter by an exceedingly large walrus washing ashore like a giant toboggan. And she thought to herself, *This is the beginning of the end.*

As he came to Auk's Landing, Lockley felt as if he'd been away for years. He felt this way because he was so homesick, so eager to see Lucy. But also because Neversink was so different from the place he had left. For one thing, the population had shrunk because of those who had recently abandoned the colony to escape the owls. The ones still here, determined to stick it out or unable to move from their nesting grounds this late in the season, seemed almost lifeless, and not just from poor nutrition. Lockley could see for himself how defeated they were.

Among the first to see him were the band of young auks led by Arne Puffin and Snorri Guillemot. "Arne!" said Lockley, "look who I brought back!" But the piffling and his friends said nothing to either Lockley or Egbert. It was as if games and play had been banished from Neversink. There was nothing to be joyous about. Lockley knew then the seas were still barren. Maybe there had been no spirit journey. Maybe it really was a dream.

Lockley tried to go immediately to his burrow, but before he got there, he ran into Algard Guillemot, who was packing his belongings. "I thought you were dead," said Algard, without sympathy. When Lockley said nothing, Algard nodded to Egbert and added, "He doesn't belong here. None of us do, anymore."

"So there has been no sign of fish?" said Lockley.

"Why would there be?" said Algard.

Before Lockley could stop him, Egbert blurted out, "Because my dear friend Lockley has just been on a spirit journey to Sedna's lair, and she has promised to restore the bounty of our waters. You should all be thanking him."

Algard did *not* thank him. In fact, what he had to say in response to this cannot be repeated here in a book for genteel and sophisticated readers. Most of the other auks within earshot muttered similarly unprintable things. Lockley was hurt, but at the moment he didn't care—he was determined to see Lucy. His heart began beating so fiercely he thought it would burst. His breath came in short, violent gulps. In part from eagerness to reunite with his beloved, yes. But Lockley realized he was also terribly afraid. Afraid of what his leaving had done to Lucy—and to them. That he was too late to save their egg. That she wouldn't forgive him.

He pushed aside the sealskin door and saw Lucy sitting

there, alone. She stood up, and said nothing as Lockley stepped inside. They just stood there, looking at each other. Lucy had been told Lockley was alive, yes. But she had not been willing to believe it fully until she saw him again. And Lockley had not been willing to believe she would be happy to see him. But then, Lucy went to him, and wrapped her wings around him. She pressed him to her and began to cry.

"I'm so happy you're back," she wept, and Lockley felt as if a stone he had been trapped under had been rolled away. His legs went weak from relief, and he began to weep as well. He stumbled back into his chair; Lucy pulled him right back up again. "There's someone you need to meet."

"In the name of Sedna!" said Lockley. "I almost forgot. . . ."

Lucy led him to their bedroom. At the threshold, Lockley paused to admire the beautiful egg, nestled in blankets. He moved toward it, and as soon as he walked through the door, he was bombarded by sharp pokes to his head and neck.

"Ow . . . ow!"

"Back off, egg snatcher!"

"Ruby, no!" cried Lucy. She had forgotten the feisty hummingbird was on guard.

When Ruby realized it was Lockley, and that he was still alive, her tiny pulse accelerated to more than a thousand beats a minute. She didn't know what to do with herself, so she flew over to Lockley, darted her tongue out, and licked his bill. "I've seen you and Lucy say hi that way," she explained to a somewhat surprised Lockley.

Lucy laughed and pulled Lockley to her again. "It's done like this," she said, and she and Lockley gently rubbed their bills together, prompting Ruby to flee the burrow.

"I think we managed to embarrass her," said Lockley.

He walked outside to tell her it was safe to come back, and as he did, he was nearly crushed by murres and razorbills coming down the walls of Auk's Landing. Circling overhead, an arctic tern was crying out, "Fish! Fish!"

It was true. A warm current had swept up from the south along Neversink's coastline. And with it, schools and schools of fish.

You have never seen such wild celebrating! Auks by the dozen plunging off the top of the sea cliffs and shore rocks after fresh eel, trout, char, cod, and other fish with short names. The burrowing owls left on Neversink who tried to stop them were trampled underfoot, their silk derbies crushed flat. All afternoon the birds feasted until happily stuffed, and then fished again just to make sure the seas were really fertile. Egbert himself ate a thousand pounds of clams. For good measure, they fished a third time just for the sake of tossing some into a pile for Rozbell—as if to say, *Tax all you want!*

You would have thought these same auks would have

come to Lockley and apologized, and given him the hero's welcome he deserved. But you'd be wrong. They all gave thanks to the Great Auk, the gods rest his soul. *He must have sacrificed his own life to appease Sedna, Rozbell, or both,* they thought. *Only an auk with the stature of the Great Auk could have accomplished such a thing.*

Lockley didn't waste energy being offended. For one thing, he was relieved that the spirit journey hadn't been just a dream. For another, he knew that the colony still had the bigger problem of a despotic little owl to contend with.

Astra once again found herself having to make the flight back to Tytonia. There wasn't another owl or messenger bird willing to personally deliver the news to Rozbell that the puffin who had deprived him of smidgens, the husband of the puffin who had humiliated him publicly, had returned safely to Neversink. She had to do it herself. And Rozbell practically invented the phrase *kill the messenger.*

To her surprise, Rozbell directed his anger at Feathertop: "You . . . incompetent . . . fool!" he screeched at the stunned eagle. The king's eyes bulged and his feathers fluffed out as if he'd received a jolt of electricity. "You were supposed to take care of this in the first place, and then you lied about it with the help of that raven! I've always said, you can't trust a raven!"

Feathertop tried to protest, looking repeatedly in Astra's

direction, but he couldn't get a word in edgewise.

"You featherbrained, feather-headed idiot! You and those overgrown blackbirds! You aren't fit to fly! You aren't fit to sit in my owlery! You ought to be plucked and paraded around the woods like a lemming! Look at you—as big as an ox and just as stupid! *Gewh, gewh, gewh!*" On and on it went, with hundreds of other choice words that were again, I regret, far too indecent for cultivated readers.

For Rozbell, Lockley's return symbolized his failure to get what he wanted, whether it was the food he craved or the power to crush the loathsome auks. His tirade went on for several more minutes, and news of his rage soon circulated throughout the territory.

On Neversink, the auks' bellies were full, but the news of Rozbell's fury gave them all indigestion (which they blamed on Lockley, of course). Lockley knew he had to think of something fast. He pulled the now empty clamshell necklace out of his breast feathers again and stared at it. Maybe there was still luck in it yet, he thought. Or maybe, just maybe, there was more luck where the clamshell came from.

He needed a quiet place to think anyway, so he made his way down the shore to the Great Auk's abandoned nest. He was relieved to see that at least someone had had respect enough to come tidy up—even put things back where they belonged, as if the nest was now a shrine to their former leader. *Here is where he kept his tea. And here is where he kept his tea cups. And here is where he boiled water for his tea.* In fact, there was a pot of water boiling now. *Well, that's going a bit far,* thought Lockley.

A voice behind him said, "Hello, Lockley."

He turned around. It was the Great Auk.

ROZBELL'S CLUTCHES

Lockley wondered if he was seeing a ghost. After his trip to Sedna's lair, anything seemed possible.

"It's really me, Lockley."

"How did you escape?"

"It's not important right now," said the Great Auk. "I trust, from the bountiful seas, that you found the biteweed useful?"

"Oh yes," said Lockley, clasping the shell again. "I can't thank you enough. I guess your foresight is as good as ever. You were spot-on about the Owls With Hats, after all."

"You don't really need to be a seer to predict that owls will make trouble, now do you?" said the Great Auk. "As for the spirit journey, I made it once, long ago. I gave you the clamshell because I felt that if the journey needed to be made again, I would be too old to do it. As you no doubt discovered, it is a trying task. I know your confidence was shaken after the fish party. I had faith, though, in your resourcefulness."

"Well, that makes one of us," said Lockley. He went on to recount his disastrous escape attempt, being fooled by a tiny mole, of all creatures, and then detailed his spirit journey. The Great Auk compared it to what he had once seen. He was intrigued by Lockley's vision of the future in the World Tree, where the apes were climbing among the birds. Lockley still had something nagging at his brain. "What about Sedna?" he wondered. "Her shape, her form . . . what is she?"

"The birds say she is made in the gods' own image," the Great Auk replied. "As the story is told, the gods were displeased with their experiment, because she was tricked by a bird. And so they made her an immortal." Lockley nodded, though he still didn't fully understand. "The gods don't give up easily," said the Great Auk. "There will soon be others."

Lockley wanted to know more, but he had a confession to make first. He admitted to the Great Auk that he hadn't really remembered the entire "Tricking of Sedna" story. That Egbert and the Scholars had to help complete the mission. The Great Auk didn't seem too angry. "Good friends come in handy, do they not? And perhaps now, with your help, we can persuade the others of the need to collect the Stories somewhere, for when our memories fail us?"

Lockley agreed, but there were more urgent matters at hand if this particular story was to have a happy ending. He told the Great Auk what Sedna had told him—that no false ruler could perch on a branch of the World Tree.

"A branch of the World Tree," said the Great Auk. After a pause he said, "I may be able to help with that." And there was a glint in his eye when he said it.

The next morning, Lockley came out of his burrow to find a crowd gathered at Auk's Landing, which wasn't all that unusual. Except that along with the families of puffins, murres, guillemots, and razorbills, there were also Owls With Hats everywhere. When Lockley spotted the menacing Feathertop and, next to him, the glint of Rozbell's new gold crown, he knew the moment of truth was at hand.

"There he is!" someone cried. The whole crowd of auks and owls re-formed into a half circle as Lockley came forward and put himself face-to-face with Rozbell, who stood on a rock to meet Lockley's eyes. Egbert went to Lockley's side. Feathertop loomed over Rozbell's shoulder with a sour look on his face.

"Well, well, well," said Rozbell. "I must admit, I thought

you had met a most unfortunate end. Just goes to show, you can't send an eagle to do an owl's job." Feathertop's expression went from merely sour to downright hideous. "Has everyone brought you up to speed? There have been a few changes around here."

"Well, *duh*," said Ruby, appearing over Egbert's head.

Lockley stepped closer. "Actually, I've had a lot of time to think on my journeys, and I'm back to offer my full support."

"You are?" said Egbert, Ruby, and Rozbell in unison.

"Quite right," said Lockley. "I've heard there's been some controversy over the change of leadership and the arrangements between Tytonia and Neversink. I think I can put an end to all that. After all, if you are the legitimate leader of the owls, then you have every right to lead as you see fit."

Rozbell smelled a rat, which for owls is normally a good thing, but not in this case. "What do you mean, *if*?"

At which point Lockley produced what looked like a crooked, bleached tree limb and held it up for all to see. "This is a branch from the World Tree!" he shouted.

There was a collective gasp, and Egbert leaned in and asked, "Where on earth did that come from?"

"Yes," said Rozbell, his eyes afire. "Where on earth did that come from?"

"I gave it to him," came a voice from the back. The crowd gasped again as the Great Auk strode forward. The auks were electrified; Rozbell looked as if he might self-combust.

"Is *anyone* I ordered killed actually dead?"

Lockley saw the Great Auk glance at Astra from the corner of his eye, although the stoic white owl betrayed nothing.

"You all remember the story," said the Great Auk. "A branch of the World Tree was passed down through descendants of each of the Birds of the Four Talents." Of course, the auks and the owls did *not* remember this story. But from the mouth of the Great Auk, it sounded authoritative enough.

"What you may not know," added Lockley, lowering his voice for dramatic effect, "is that no illegitimate ruler may perch in the World Tree."

The shore was now abuzz, and Rozbell was livid. A fit of spastic blinking overcame him. Blinking and fuming, he turned back to Lockley. "I don't see a tree anywhere," he spat. "All I see is a miserable little stump!"

"Don't be so hard on yourself," said Ruby.

"This *stump*, as you call it, is a part of a whole that still exists in spirit," said Lockley. "If you are legitimate, you will be able to clutch the branch in your talons, and then I give you my word that Neversink will not question your authority."

Evidently Lockley had not consulted the other auks

about this, because his promise provoked a great deal of hissing and growling. But when they looked to the Great Auk, he nodded in agreement.

"And what, pray tell, supposedly happens if I am *not* legitimate?" said Rozbell. "Just out of curiosity."

"You will die," said Lockley.

"Why should I believe anything a *fish-eater* tells me about the World Tree?"

"Then believe me," said an aged voice, this one from Rozbell's camp. Heads spun around to find that Otus, the elderly scops owl, had spoken. "The puffin is quite correct," he said.

"He's one of the king's old lackeys!" Rozbell snapped. "You can't trust him." But all eyes, both owl and auk, stayed fixed on Rozbell and Lockley.

Lockley held out the branch. "Well?"

Rozbell looked from Lockley to the branch and back to Lockley again. Then he let out a shrill hoot. "I don't have time for your insolence. My authority is already unquestioned."

Much to Rozbell's surprise, his own camp seemed dissatisfied with this answer. Otus came forward and said, "I, for one, would be interested to see what happens."

"Who cares what you think?" said Rozbell.

But then two large eagle owls swooped down and stood before Rozbell. "We'd like to see what happens as well," they said coldly. "Take the branch." The other owls crowded closer.

Rozbell was cornered. Everyone knew how he had come to power. The question of his legitimacy was irrelevant. But if he refused to clutch the branch, he would look like a coward. And his paranoid mind told him there were plenty among his followers who would exploit any show of weakness to seize the crown. But if he clutched the branch and the World Tree myth was true . . .

With all eyes on him, Rozbell lifted one leg off the ground and gently pressed the bottom of his foot against the branch. Slowly, his talons closed around it. When nothing happened, he carefully brought his other foot forward, until he was fully perched on the branch.

No one moved or uttered a peep. Rozbell looked down at his feet, as if to be sure he was really perched there. Then, surging with a furious confidence, he pointed to Lockley, the Great Auk, and Otus, and said to Feathertop, "Kill them all!"

Instead, a most unexpected thing happened.

The great white form of Astra swooped down and snatched Rozbell from the branch as if she were picking fruit off a tree, and bore the little tyrant off over the water.

"*Feathertop!*" cried a tiny voice in the wind, but while the martial eagle did launch himself into the air, he did not chase after his master. Rather, he banked to the south, presumably headed for the much warmer climate of his African home. Everyone else just stood there, bills agape, until both the snowy owl and the martial eagle were specks on the horizon.

"I didn't see that coming," said Ruby.

"Fascinating," was all Egbert could muster.

Lockley turned to the Great Auk and smiled. Behind them an unseen voice from the owls' camp whispered, "The World Tree!" And in no time, the sentiment picked up steam until it was agreed upon that justice had been served, and an illegitimate ruler had been banished.

The owls gathered near Otus, and one of the Owls With Hats removed his derby and looked it over curiously, as if he had just discovered the strange object on his head. "These things seem a bit ridiculous on a bird, don't they?" he said. There was a murmur of agreement, and others began removing their hats and looking them over, as if reconsidering their worth. Otus then led the whole group in flight back to Tytonia. It was quite a sight, and if one paid attention, one could see hats being tossed into the sea as the owls made their way home.

The auks gathered around the Great Auk and welcomed him home, eager to hear what had happened with him and Sedna. Most were skeptical when he insisted they had Lockley to thank for their reversal of fortune. "I'm not getting younger, stronger, or even wiser," he explained.

"That's why I let Lockley confront Rozbell. It's about time you all started thinking about someone who could succeed me."

Lockley could tell the other auks thought the Great Auk had gone completely mental. He even thought he heard a laughing gull cackling in the distance. Eventually the auks returned to their burrows, to get back to the business of minding their own business. Algard Guillemot walked up to Lockley, lifted his bill slightly, and grunted, which Lockley knew was a sign of grudging respect.

As for Lockley, Egbert, and Ruby, the three friends lingered after everyone else wandered away, beaming at one another. It had crossed each of their minds during their trials that they could have been separated forever, and the three of them might have attempted a group hug if it weren't physically impossible for a puffin, a walrus, and a hummingbird to embrace.

Finally Lockley said, "I guess I should be getting home to Lucy," and he tossed the World Tree branch into the surf.

"Good heavens, what are you doing?" said Egbert.

"Oh, that. That was just an old piece of driftwood. We Arctic birds are a tricky lot. Just add Rozbell to the long list of birds and beasts to underestimate us!"

"But . . ."

"No one takes mythology to heart more than an owl," said Lockley. "You taught me that, old boy. It was all worked out between the Great Auk, Astra, and me. If Rozbell had been too afraid to clutch the branch, it would have been as good as surrendering. But by calling our bluff, he essentially gave Astra permission to attack him, since everyone knew he was illegitimate."

"I don't know what to say," said Egbert.

"You don't? This truly *is* a remarkable day!" said Ruby.

"A remarkable summer," said Lockley.

The vanquishing of Rozbell led to changes aplenty on Neversink and Tytonia. The owls anointed Otus their new king, but created the position of prime minister so that no one owl would have absolute authority. To the Great Auk's delight, Astra was elected the first prime minister, and her first official task was to meet with the Great Auk about restoring and improving the Peace of Yore. More importantly, they forged a new treaty: the Great Auk made the same promise he had made to Rozbell—to supply raw fish to Tytonia until it was determined that the owls' food supply was no longer threatened.

There was also a proper ceremony of mourning for those who had lost their eggs to the owls, and in an unexpected show of determination, those bereaved families agreed it wasn't too late in the breeding season to try again.

But in a melancholy twist for Lockley, Egbert returned to Ocean's End. His former clan had learned of his bravery in the face of the White Death, and they invited him to return. The Scholars, too, after much deliberation, Unshunned him, and offered him a position, on a trial basis, as Associate Scholar of Less-Ancient History. "It's quite unprecedented for them to create a new post," Egbert explained. "An immense honor. Of course, it will be a nonvoting position."

Egbert was torn about leaving Neversink again, especially with Lockley back and peace restored. But Lockley gave him his blessing: "You deserve the chance to go home, old friend."

Soon the sun began to dip below the horizon, heralding the end of summer on Neversink, which meant that Lockley would lose Ruby too, at least for the winter. One morning, while taking tea with Lucy, Ruby flew into their burrow and told Lockley she needed him right away.

Ruby asked Lockley to close his eyes and follow the sound of her wings, but the path along which she led him was full of rocks and dips, and Lockley kept losing his balance. "Ruby, what the devil!"

"Not much farther," she promised, and then finally, on the other side of the sea cliffs, she let him open his eyes. They were on a grassy plain near where Egbert had held his birthday party—what seemed like ages ago. When they crested the last hill, Lockley saw a sight that made his eyes well up with tears. It was Egbert, busy ordering a number of other strange animals around.

"Ta-da!" said Ruby.

"Lockley, my dear," said Egbert, as if he had never been gone, "don't ever try to build your own library!"

"I wasn't planning to, but . . . Egbert! You're back? But . . ."

"Enough *buts*, my dear. I merely took your advice to heart."

"What advice?"

"You told me I deserved a chance to go home. And as I once told a certain sadistic owl, Neversink is my home."

Still blinking away tears, Lockley asked, "So what's going on here, old boy?"

"The Scholars were right," said Egbert. "I've never taken to heart their belief that knowledge is the domain of a privileged few. So I'm building my own library, right here on Neversink. For *everyone*."

Lockley remembered his trip inside the Scholars' library, and although Egbert wasn't using ivory and ice, his library was most definitely taking a similar shape. Two giant beavers had floated timber from the mainland and were measuring and cutting all the beams and joists. An army of carpenter ants was raising and lashing all the pieces. Mud wasps were filling in the walls. And an industrious pair of weaverbirds flown in from Africa were thatching together the roof.

Amazed at the progress, Lockley asked, "How long have

you been back exactly?"

"I tell you," said Ruby, "keeping a chatty walrus under wraps is no easy task!"

The three old friends spent the next several hours enjoying the reunion they had been deprived of when Egbert was invited back to Ocean's End. Talk inevitably turned to owls, hats, Sedna, tyranny, and redemption and all the rest, and Egbert tried to explain the moral of the story that nearly saw Neversink come to ruin.

"My dear Lockley, this adventure has undoubtedly taught you to appreciate the difference between things you *can* change, and those you can't."

"No it hasn't," said Ruby. "He's still embarrassed by his ridiculous bill and his wobbly little body."

"Well . . . ," said Lockley.

"You haven't been trying to *soar* again, have you, my dear?"

"No," Lockley said firmly. "Puffins don't soar. Not like that, anyway."

Egbert nodded his approval, but Ruby wasn't done. "And besides, Rozbell was able to change Neversink—for the worse!"

"I suppose," said Egbert. "Well then, I think we've all learned that you should stand up for what you believe in, no matter what the consequences."

"But didn't Rozbell do that?" said Ruby. "He really

believed he should be king, and everyone else suffered the consequences."

Egbert's face was turning quite pink. "Then the moral is, Being good is its own reward!"

"What about all the suffering?"

"Well then, Knowledge is power!"

"Just because you're smart means you can't abuse power?"

"Oh, for the love of fish!"

Lockley felt certain this could go on for some time. The familiar, bickering voices of his friends warmed his heart. But just now, he wasn't in the mood to sort out the meaning of it all, and so he slipped away quietly. He intended to go home, have a nice dinner with his wife, and hold his newborn piffling under his wings.

But first he went to the outskirts of Auk's Landing, to that narrow ledge that jutted out over the sea—the place where he used to dream of soaring. Lockley stood there in silence over the corrugated-tin sea, watching the water accelerate and collide with the shore, crumpling against the rocks. He took in the briny air and the scent of fish, and listened to the gulls and terns laughing and cheering and squabbling with the auks and seals, and he thought what a fine, late summer day it was, indeed.

THE END

Neversink

The Mythology of Neversink

The Fact Behind the Fiction,
or Infrequently Asked Questions

Sam Nielson's Sketchbook

The Mythology of Neversink

At the center of the birds' cosmos is the World Tree, a sacred motif in many religions, including those of Native Americans, Indo-European cultures like the Norse (*Yggdrasil*), and Hindus (*Ashvattha,* the Sacred Fig). In all cases, it seems, the tree grows through and connects the various realms of heaven, earth, and underworld. And really, why wouldn't birds have a World Tree?

Sedna, the Mother of the Sea, is also borrowed from religion. She was worshipped as the goddess of the sea and marine animals by the Inuit, the indigenous peoples of the Arctic regions of Greenland, Canada, the United States, and Russia. The first time I read the story of her being tricked by a bird and being vengeful and unpredictable, I knew she would make the perfect goddess for seafaring, fish-eating birds like auks.

Personally, I like to think humans got all these ideas from animals, and that *Neversink* just properly reorders the time line.

The Fact Behind the Fiction or, Infrequently Asked Questions

Can owls really make hats?

I maintain that if birds can build nests, they can make hats. Plus, I liked inventing a plausible story for how the first crown came into being.

Did walruses really invent writing?

Yes. Maybe. Who knows? We humans take credit for so much. According to legend, the Chinese scribe Cangjie invented writing after observing the marks left on the ground by birds. Who says that birds weren't making those marks intentionally? Chicken scratch might be literature right under our feet. Regardless, that story inspired the idea of walruses inventing a written language based on their hide scars. And I for one would love to visit the Walrus Library at Ocean's End and peruse one of the great ice sagas myself.

A hummingbird near the Arctic Circle? Impossible!

Well, I did explain that Ruby ended up there by accident, and only hangs around during the warmest periods. But it's a mistake to think we know all there is to know about animal behavior past and present. The rufous hummingbird summers in Alaska. And though we have always assumed that hummingbirds evolved in South America, thirty-million-year-old hummingbird fossils were unearthed not too long ago in Germany. This primitive hummingbird species has been named Eurotrochilus inexpectatus, which sounds like a Harry Potter curse but really is just Latin for "unexpected European hummingbird." Unexpected, indeed.

Are auks real? Really?

I had a college professor who talked about how Charles Dickens had a few tricks up his sleeve for creating his famously larger-than-life characters: funny or suggestive names; exaggerated physical traits; expressive gestures or speech patterns. Well, with animals, most of that work is done for you. I mean, just look at the puffin! It looks like something Lewis Carroll would have invented for Wonderland if it didn't already exist. An owl that's basically a head on legs? Hummingbirds and walruses?

Herewith my main cast of characters, and how the real world inspired my fantasy one.

Lockley Puffin: Puffins really do nest at or below ground level, are relatively small and silent compared to their auk cousins, and seem to be aware of how funny-looking they are. All classic traits of a reluctant-hero type in my book. Sort of like a Hobbit with wings.

Rozbell: Pygmy owls are the smallest owl species in that part of the world, and are ambush hunters (in other words, sneaky). Many villains in world history were men compensating for a lack of physical strength and stature (hence the term "Napoleon complex"), and I liked the idea of Rozbell clawing and conniving his way to power in a might-makes-right animal kingdom. He's crazy, but he has a legitimate ax to grind with the tradition of owl leadership.

Ruby and Egbert: I love physical comedy, as well as the grand tradition of comedy buddy teams, like Laurel and Hardy, Don

Quixote and Sancho Panza, or the huge bulldog and his tiny, yappy sidekick from the Bugs Bunny cartoons, to name a few. There always seems to be a dramatic size difference that contributes to the way their personalities and dialogue are foils for each other. The idea of a walrus and a hummingbird together—one large in every way, including his ego, and the other tiny, tireless, and feisty—just made me laugh.

As for the story itself, when I learned that the collective noun for owls is parliament, and puffins are sometimes called a colony, it suggested a political allegory to me, but one rooted in the natural world. Both Tytonia, the woodsy domain of the governing owls, and the rugged, wintry sea cliffs of Neversink are true to the needs of the creatures who inhabit them, and the physical conflict is grounded in the idea that creatures are adapted to certain habitats, food supplies, and behavior cycles, and there are serious consequences if this interdependence is jeopardized.

SAM NIELSON'S SKETCHBOOK

Lockley Puffin

Ruby
6

Egbert

Other auks and owls
8

Various early interior sketches

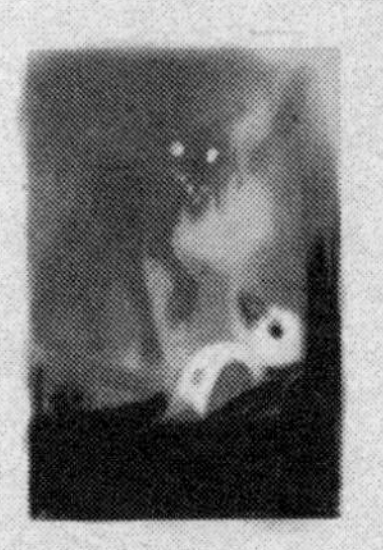

Line-style studies